THE THING ABOUT

Also by Cynthia Kadohata

*Cracker! The Best Dog in Vietnam*
*Kira-Kira*
*A Million Shades of Gray*
*Outside Beauty*
*Weedflower*

CYNTHIA KADOHATA

# THE THING ABOUT LUCK

ILLUSTRATED BY JULIA KUO

Atheneum Books for Young Readers

atheneum   New York  London  Toronto  Sydney  New Delhi

atheneum

ATHENEUM BOOKS FOR YOUNG READERS
An imprint of Simon & Schuster Children's Publishing Division
1230 Avenue of the Americas, New York, New York 10020

ATHENEUM BOOKS FOR YOUNG READERS is a registered trademark
of Simon & Schuster, Inc.
Atheneum logo is a trademark of Simon & Schuster, Inc.
For information about special discounts for bulk purchases,
please contact Simon & Schuster Special Sales at 1-866-506-1949
or business@simonandschuster.com.
The Simon & Schuster Speakers Bureau can bring authors
to your live event. For more information or to book an event, contact
the Simon & Schuster Speakers Bureau at 1-866-248-3049
or visit our website at www.simonspeakers.com.
Book design by Mike Rosamilia
The text for this book is set in Berkeley Oldstyle Book.
Manufactured in the United States of America
0513 FFG
First Edition
2 4 6 8 10 9 7 5 3 1
Library of Congress Cataloging-in-Publication Data
Kadohata, Cynthia.
The thing about luck / Cynthia Kadohata ; illustrated by Julia Kuo. — 1st ed.
p. cm.
Summary: Just when twelve-year-old Summer thinks nothing else can
possibly go wrong in a year of bad luck, an emergency takes her parents
to Japan, leaving Summer to care for her little brother while helping
her grandmother cook for harvest workers.
ISBN 978-1-4169-1882-0
ISBN 978-1-4424-7467-3 (eBook)
[1. Farm life—Kansas—Fiction. 2. Grandparents—Fiction.
3. Brothers and sisters—Fiction. 4. Japanese Americans—Fiction.
5. Luck—Fiction. 6. Kansas—Fiction.] I. Kuo, Julia, ill. II. Title.
PZ7.K1166Thi 2013
[Fic]—dc23    2012021287

FOR SAMMY,
ALWAYS AND FOREVER

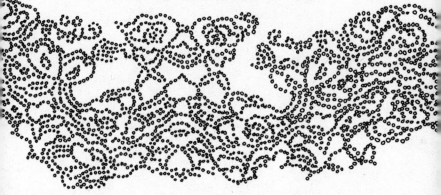

# ACKNOWLEDGMENTS

I'm deeply indebted to George Miyamoto for his big, big heart and also to Caitlyn Dlouhy—I'm quite certain there is no better editor than her in New York. Thanks as well to everyone at Simon & Schuster, including publisher Justin Chanda; Ariel Colletti; Russell Gordon, who creates such glorious covers; and managing editor extraordinaire Jeannie Ng. I'm also indebted to überagent Gail Hochman and to copy editor Cindy Nixon, who has been keeping me out of trouble for almost ten years.

Two harvesters were of incalculable help: Wendy and Taff Hughes, including their kids Shiani, Mikey, and Zeb, as well as all of Hughes Custom Harvesting, who let me visit with them in Kansas; showed me around Childress, Texas; *annnnd* let me badger them constantly—talk about generous! Jenna Zeorian of Zeorian Harvesting spoke with me, patiently answered numerous e-mails, and read the manuscript multiple times. Are all harvesters this wonderful?

I'd also like to express appreciation for others who helped me with the research for this book.

In alphabetical order: Dr. Lisa Blum, child psychologist; mosquito expert Richard Lampman, PhD, Entomology; Irish combine driver Rob Langley; Reiko Lee, who read the whole manuscript to check my Japanese; Yuki Nyhan, who also helped with the Japanese; Cyrene Puccio, who once caught malaria and who shared her experiences with me; Keith Sharpe, who, like Rob, checked the Irish idioms; and Japanese speaker Asako Suzuki.

—C. K.

# THE THING ABOUT
# LUCK

# CHAPTER ONE

*Kouun* is "good luck" in Japanese, and one year my family had none of it. We were cursed with bad luck. Bad luck chased us around, pointing her bony finger. We got seven flat tires in six weeks. I got malaria, one of fifteen hundred cases in the United States that year. And my grandmother's spine started causing her excruciating pain.

Furthermore, random bad smells emanated from we knew not where. And my brother, Jaz, became cursed with invisibility. Nobody noticed him except us. His best friend had moved away, and he did not know a single boy to hang around with. Even our cousins looked the other way when they saw him at our annual Christmas party. They didn't even seem to be snubbing my brother; they just didn't see him.

The thing about luck is that it's like a fever. You can take fever meds and lie in bed and drink chicken broth and sleep seventeen hours in a row, but basically your fever will break when it wants to break.

In early April my parents got a call from Japan. Three elderly relatives were getting ready to die and wanted my parents to take care of them in their last weeks and months. There was nothing surprising about this. This was just the way our year was going. It was April 25 when my grandparents and Jaz delivered my parents to the airport to catch their plane to Japan. I stayed at home because the type of malaria I'd gotten was called "airport malaria." Airport malaria is when a rogue mosquito from, say, Africa has been inadvertently carried into the United States on a jet. This infected mosquito might bite you. I got bit in Florida last summer, and I lived in Kansas. The chances that I would get malaria from going to the airport in Kansas were remote, but I'd grown so scared of mosquitoes that sometimes I didn't even like stepping outside. It really wasn't fair—I was only twelve, and yet already I was scared of the entire outside world.

During the 1940s there were thousands of malaria cases in the United States. Then in the fifties the experts thought malaria here was eradicated. But every so often, someone still caught it. Sometimes you would get your picture in the newspaper. My picture was even in *Time* magazine!

Obaachan and Jiichan, my grandmother and grandfather on my mother's side, were both sixty-seven and lived with us in Littlefield, Kansas. "Obaachan" was more formal than "Baachan," but it was what she wanted Jaz and me to call her.

When harvest season arrived in May of our horrible year, Jiichan planned to come out of retirement to work as a combine driver for a custom harvesting company called Parker Harvesting, Inc. (I'll explain about custom harvesting in a minute or two.) My grandmother would work as a cook for the same harvester, with me as her helper.

We'd all worked for the Parkers before. But it was the first time my parents wouldn't be there, which meant only my grandparents would be paying the mortgage during harvest this year. I didn't quite understand what "paying the mortgage" meant, but apparently, it was a constant struggle. Another phrase that came up a lot was "paying down the principal," as in, "If we could just pay down the principal, I'd feel like we were getting somewhere." I used to think that "paying down the principal" meant they wanted to bribe the principal at one of my future schools, like they would give this principal some money, and then someday the principal would let me into high school despite my iffy grades.

Anyway. As soon as my grandparents got home from dropping off my parents, changes were implemented. My mother had told Jaz, "Don't worry. You'll make a friend when you least expect it." My grandparents were more proactive. It seems Obaachan and Jiichan had a bright idea they'd been hiding from us.

Obaachan made Jaz and me sit on the floor in front of the coffee table while she and Jiichan sat on the couch. "We having meeting-party," she announced regally. "We invite boys we will consider for friendship with Jaz." She turned to me. "Make list with him. I no interfere."

"A list of people to invite?" I asked. My Doberman, Thunder, tried to push himself between me and the table. I pushed back, and we just sat there, leaning hard into each other.

"No! A list!" she snapped at me.

Wasn't that what I had just said? I finally got up and moved to a different side of the table. Still unsure what she wanted, I got a pen and paper.

"Pencil! You may need to erase."

I got a pencil and readied myself. "Should I number the list?" I asked.

My grandfather nodded sagely. "Agenda," he said. "List for boys we invite, agenda for party."

"No interfere!" Obaachan said to Jiichan.

"You interfere first!"

"No!"

Obaachan and Jiichan had been married for forty-nine years, and my mother always said that after that number of years, you no longer had to be polite all the time. It sometimes seemed that in our house, I was the only one who had to use my manners. Jaz didn't have to because he had issues. When I'm sixty-seven, in fifty-five years, I supposed that I would finally be able to dispense with my manners.

I thought Jiichan and Obaachan talked to each other the way that they did because they'd had an arranged marriage. Obaachan said that if I had an arranged marriage, I would never give or receive a broken heart. If I grew up beautiful, I would never break any man's heart, and if I grew up plain, nobody would break my heart. If I rebelled and wanted love, however, all bets were off. Broken hearts would come my way like locusts.

"Summer! You in rah-rah land." She never said "la-la land," and I never corrected her.

I hurriedly wrote *Number one* on the paper in the left-hand margin.

"No number," Obaachan said. "Arrange by time. I have to tell you everything?"

Jiichan picked up the paper, studied the *Number one*, and set the paper back down. "I agree. Arrange by time."

I erased the *Number one* and wrote in *One o'clock p.m.* I made sure not to flick the eraser bits onto the floor, because if I did, Obaachan would be so upset that she might fall over dead.

"Noon!" barked Obaachan. I made the change. "Continue. First write day on top of paper in big letter. Day for meeting is next Saturday. Then continue."

"What would you like to do at noon?" I asked Jaz.

"Play with LEGOs. I want a LEGO party."

"Not really party," Jiichan said. He was cleaning his teeth with the floss he always carried in his shirt pocket. Sometimes he flossed during dinner, right at the table. See what I mean about manners? Can you imagine what your parents would do if you started to floss at the dinner table? But he constantly seemed to have something between his teeth. "More of meeting than party," he said.

"Noon lunchtime," Obaachan said. "You feed boys first. Boys always hungry. Never mind. I no interfere. But no food, no friend. What I just say?"

"No food, no friend," Jaz and I repeated.

7

Obaachan sometimes made us repeat something she had just said, to prove we were listening.

Jaz turned to Obaachan. "Obaachan, will you make sandwiches?"

"Summer make. I her mentor."

I found myself already starting to feel stressed. What if I made ham sandwiches and the boys wanted tuna fish? What if I used regular bread and one of the boys needed gluten-free, like my friend Alyssa had to eat because of her allergies? What if I used too much mayonnaise? Arghhh!

Still, next to *Noon* I wrote *Sandwich eating*.

Jiichan pounded on the paper. "Lunch!" he cried out passionately. "Not 'sandwich eating'! It called 'lunch'!" He clutched at his heart. "You kids go to kill me." Apparently, about once every couple of weeks, he thought we were going to kill him.

"What kind of sandwiches would you like?" I asked Jaz, still worrying about those. "I don't want to make the wrong kind."

"I'll ask around at school. I can't believe this is happening. I'm really going to have a meeting-party." He got up to look at himself in a mirror over our fake fireplace and said, "You are going to have a meeting-party."

Jiichan was now standing and staggering away from us with his hands on his heart. Jaz and I watched him calmly. "I die, scatter ashes," Jiichan said. "No keep in hole in wall at cemetery. You hear me?"

"Yes, Jiichan," we said.

"Good. Then I die happy."

I wrote down *LEGOs, one o'clock*. My brother had approximately one thousand dollars' worth of LEGOs. Seriously. I counted once. LEGOs were one of our biggest expenses and the only thing we splurged on.

"Good plan!" Jiichan said. "That brilliant!" I couldn't tell if he was being sarcastic as he peered over my shoulder from his death throes.

"How long is the meeting-party?" Jaz asked.

"I think most parties are two hours," I answered. "So I guess that's the end of the agenda?" Nobody answered, so I made a line underneath the agenda and laid down the pencil.

"Who should I invite?" Jaz asked. "Should it be just kids who I think might come, or should it be kids who might not come but on the other hand you never know? Should it be just kids in my class, or should it be all the kids in my grade? Should it be boys and girls or just boys? Should it be only kids who might not even know who I am even though I know who they are? Should it—"

Jiichan held up his palm to quiet Jaz. "Invite whole fifth grade," he said wisely. We all looked at him, and he nodded. "That way hurt nobody's feelings."

Jaz stared at him doubtfully for a moment, but then his face turned from doubtful to ecstatic. I could almost hear him thinking, *Wow, the whole school might come to my meeting-party!*

Then my grandparents wanted Jaz to draw invitations. He was a good artist in kind of a weird way. Like, he never drew pictures of anything recognizable, but if you needed a totally psychedelic design, he was your man. But he wanted to buy invitations because he thought they were more official. We ended up driving thirty miles to a 99-cent store in a larger town. After loud and passionate debate, we bought several boxes of dinosaur invitations. On Monday,

Jaz distributed them to all the kids in the fifth grade at his school.

So as not to jinx the party, we weren't supposed to talk to one another about it. But we could pray all we wanted, in front of several sprigs of silk cherry blossoms on the coffee table. We did this the night before the party. Cherry blossoms, as the harbingers of spring, were important to Japanese farmers. My grandmother mumbled in Japanese as I knelt beside her. I could make out a word occasionally—like *unmei* for "destiny."

As Obaachan muttered on, I prayed in my head: *Please let my brother have a successful meeting-party. Let the kids have fun, let him make at least one friend, preferably two. Please, please, please.*

That night I drew in my notebook like I always did. I didn't draw very well, so each picture took me weeks. I copied them from photographs of mosquitoes I found.

One time I thought I had a perfect drawing, so I sent it to a mosquito expert, and this is what he said: "Looks like an Anopheles, but the proboscis is 'hairy' and the palps look like a thin line, so this is not a good representation, but could easily

11

be changed (make palps more than a line and get rid of bristle on mouthparts and you have an Anopheles female). The problem is that most (but not all) Anopheles in the U.S. tend to have spots on their wings, which these drawings lack." Wow, epic fail on my part!

It was strange because I knew that if I had almost been killed by a car, I wouldn't have become fascinated with cars. If I had almost drowned, I wouldn't have become obsessed with water. But the more I looked at mosquitoes, even the same type that had infected me, the more delicate they seemed. Fragile, even. And yet one had almost taken my life. It was like now we couldn't be separated. I mean, if I saw one on my arm, I wouldn't hesitate to smash it or even run screaming down the highway. They terrified me. But still, we were inseparable.

# CHAPTER TWO

Three boys from Jaz's class had said they could come to the party. Nobody else had RSVP'd. But it didn't matter. Three boys! We were so, so excited. At eleven on Saturday morning my friend Melody came over in case we needed help.

"What should I do?" Mel asked Obaachan.

"Vacuum living room."

"Obaachan," I said, "she's a guest."

"She here to work."

I shook my head at Mel to let her know she didn't have to vacuum. But we couldn't have a for-real conversation with Obaachan and Jiichan listening. So we just talked about the coming harvest.

Let me finally explain about custom harvesters. Many wheat farmers don't cut their own wheat. They bring in custom harvesters like the Parkers, who hire independent contractors like my family to drive the giant combines that cut the wheat. They also hire drivers of big rigs to haul the wheat to grain elevators. Grain elevators are usually tall reinforced-concrete buildings that you may have seen but never really thought about. The elevators are where the grain is stored.

The custom harvesters are the ones who own or lease the really, really expensive equipment. They're usually family-owned companies. A new combine can cost $350,000, so you need to have really good credit to get a loan from the bank to buy or lease your equipment. Shoot, our house cost a quarter of that. During the harvest season these companies travel from farm to farm, from Texas to Montana or North Dakota, and even up to Canada for some harvesters.

Anyway, enough about custom harvesters (for now). I made two chicken-breast sandwiches, and Mel made two. Every so often, I slipped Thunder a piece of chicken, so he sat his best sit as I cut the sandwiches in half and inserted toothpicks topped with colored cellophane into each half. Then I put a sprig of parsley on each plate, which is kind of fancy, but I wanted to make a good impression.

Melody, Obaachan, Jiichan, and I sat at the kitchen table waiting while Jaz sat in the living room. "Summer, get your hair under control," Obaachan said. "You look like Yoko Ono, 1969." I had the bad luck of being in that small minority of Asian people with frizzy hair. Usually I wore it in braids, but I hadn't done that today.

I braided my hair in the bathroom. Melody came with me. "I have a bad feeling about this whole party thing," I said.

"What do you mean?" Mel asked.

"I don't know. At least we're going on harvest pretty soon. Kids are less snotty on harvest. They're desperate for someone to play with. Me, I'm mostly worried that everyone at school will forget me."

"I won't forget you if you promise you won't forget me," Mel said.

"Deal," I said.

"Deal," she responded.

So at least I would have one friend to come back to. We hadn't gone on harvest the previous year because my parents had found local work, so this would be my first harvest since I got sick. Lately, I'd been lying in bed at night, thinking on the one hand, about all the mosquitoes I would see on harvest, and on the other hand, what it would do to my health to be smearing on the insecticide DEET every night for several months. Supposedly, DEET was known for not being bad for humans, but whenever I first put it on, Thunder didn't like to be near me.

With my hair braided, Mel and I checked on Jaz in the living room. He was sitting on the couch wearing his favorite T-shirt, which was neon green. When noon came and went, I put the plates into the refrigerator. I went to check on Jaz again. His hands were folded in his lap, and he was staring straight ahead. There was no clock in the living room, so he may not have known that it was ten after twelve.

Back at the kitchen table, we waited some more. At twenty past noon Obaachan said, "Why say come when no come? Why say yes when mean no?"

I looked down at the flecks of silver in the kitchen table. Jaz had once counted every fleck on the table; there were 3,412. That was just the kind of boy he was, and that was why he had no friends.

I went to peek at my brother again. His hands were still folded in his lap, but now his jaw was hanging open. My brother was small and stocky, like a four-foot tall weight lifter. He was built exactly like my grandfather, a rectangle with a head on top. It was disconcerting to talk to Jaz because his eyes had a strange, unwavering quality. He was a very serious kiddo, but I had seen him smile. I had heard him laugh. So I knew he could be happy sometimes.

I started to feel furious at the boys in Jaz's class. Were they completely heartless? Finally, at 12:45, my grandmother's back slumped with defeat. I had never seen her like this before. Jiichan flossed his teeth, as if nothing special were going on.

"What Jaz doing?" Obaachan asked.

"Just sitting in the living room with his mouth hanging open," I answered. "He's hardly moved."

At one o'clock, my grandfather laid down his floss and declared, "Nobody coming. Let's eat sandwich. Let's celebrate, ah, we can celebrate, ah . . ."

Nobody could think of anything to celebrate, so Jiichan just got to his feet and took the sandwiches out of the fridge. "Go get your brother."

I walked reluctantly into the living room, where Jaz sat stoically. "Jiichan says we should eat." Then I said it again.

He looked at his feet. "Why doesn't anybody like me?" he asked.

I thought of saying, *You have a bad temper, and you're weird.* He had such a bad temper that when he was angry, he sometimes banged his head on a wall or on whatever was handy. And he was weird because he would do strange things. Like, one time when he started singing a song in the middle of a test. My mother loved to tell that story because she thought it was cute, but I doubted the kids in his class thought it was cute. But I knew now wasn't the time for honesty. "You had a friend, but he moved away. That wasn't your fault. You'll make another one."

"Connor Foster smells, and he even brags that

he takes only one bath a week, and even he has a couple of friends," Jaz went on, now looking at me directly.

I hated all the boys in Jaz's class. In my class the boys were nicer. They did not shun anyone. But then I remembered Jenson, who didn't have a single friend that I knew of. I had rarely given him a thought, but now my heart went out to him. He was long and lanky, and he always held his chin slightly up, so you could see in his nostrils. And, it was hard to explain, but there was something about him that kind of repelled everyone. It was something about the way he moved, not in smooth, normal strokes like most people, but rather kind of jerky, as if he were part robot. Right then and there, I vowed to say something to him one day. Even if it was only "hello," it would acknowledge that he was there.

Jaz stood up. "Okay, let's eat."

Everybody took half a sandwich, along with some potato chips. We ate silently. Jaz was a focused eater, just as he was focused with about everything he did. He stared down his food as if eating were a fight to the finish, and he chewed so vigorously that my parents worried he might crack his teeth.

"Boys need red meat to grow, not chicken," Obaachan finally said, not sharply, but weakly, as if she had been defeated today. I think she loved Jaz more than she loved me, but at that moment I didn't mind. Jaz needed all the love he could get.

# CHAPTER THREE

Nothing more happened as far as making friends for Jaz. But a few weeks later, as I walked into class on my last day before we left for harvest, for some reason, my eyes rested on Jenson. I remembered vowing to say hello to him, so I cheerfully called out, "Hi, Jenson." Several people looked at me like, *What are you doing saying hello to Jenson of all people? Jenson?*

Jenson glared at me suspiciously, then said, "Shut up."

Wow. I didn't expect that. People were still looking at me, and I felt my face grow hot. I thought about what Jenson had just said. He must have been incredibly lonely to respond that way.

I heard one boy saying to another, "Hey, Summer likes Jenson."

Even though I knew Jenson was lonely, now I was annoyed at him. "I was just trying to be friendly," I called out.

"And I was just trying to say shut up," Jenson shot back.

And now everybody was laughing at me. I knew nobody would remember any of this in September when I got back; still, when I took my seat, my face was burning.

I got called on four times that day. I had to solve an equation with two unknowns on the board, read a page out loud, explain what an element was, and define "ethical" versus "moral." Boy, I was glad to be free when the bell rang.

After school I walked with some friends to where the school bus stopped. The ones who didn't take the bus hugged me good-bye. When the bus came, I sat next to Melody as usual. Then I don't know what possessed me, but I wanted to try to be nice to Jenson one more time. He was sitting alone, as if people were scared that if they sat next to him, some of his unpopularity might rub off on them, which it probably would. But I figured I had loyal friends, so I could afford to lose a couple of popularity points. I got up, walked straight back, and sat right there next to him. I felt his leg against mine, so I moved over a bit in the opposite direction.

"We're going away for harvest tomorrow," I said pleasantly.

He looked at me with annoyance and said, "You again?"

"Yeah, I just wanted to sit here and, like . . . talk or something." I saw several kids, including Jaz, watching me curiously. I couldn't think of what to say next. I finally came up with, "I like your shirt," which was a ridiculous thing to say because his shirt was heavy plaid flannel, even though it was warm out.

He thought a second. "I don't know what's going on, but I've known you since first grade, and I don't think you've ever spoken a word to me. So thanks for whatever you're trying to do, but bug off."

Well. That hadn't turned out very agreeably.

Then we came to my stop, and my friends were hugging me and we were saying good-bye.

"See you!" I called out before I stepped off of the bus.

When I turned to head home, Thunder was sitting near the bush where he always waited for me. I walked with him a ways, then stopped in the middle of a bunch of weeds and sat down and rolled my head around to stretch my neck. I felt all tense. I didn't know why.

"What are you doing?" Jaz said behind me. At least people didn't mind sitting next to him. In that way, he was better off than Jenson.

"I'm de-stressing," I said. De-stressing was what my dad did all the time. For instance, if you bothered him while he was watching sports on TV, he'd say, "Not now, honey, I'm de-stressing."

Jaz shrugged and walked toward our house.

After de-stressing, I went inside. Jiichan had stretched a big map across the kitchen table to show us our route. This season we would be traveling from Texas to Oklahoma, back to Kansas, to Colorado, and to the Dakotas. If there was one thing I hated, it was road trips. It wasn't that I found road trips boring. It was just that I would be trapped with my grandmother and Jaz for hours at a time. I mean, I loved them, but thinking of spending all that time with them made me crazy. My grandfather was different. I could ride with him all day, no problem.

For me, taking off time from school would be sort of wonderful and awful at the same time—wonderful because I hated schoolwork, and awful because my mother had told me that a lot would change for my entire class over the summer between sixth and seventh grades. And whatever these changes were, I wouldn't be there for them. When we studied the civil rights movement that took place about a hundred thousand years earlier in the 1960s, we heard Sam Cooke singing "A Change Is Gonna Come," which was my favorite song in the world, or at least my second favorite. I didn't have a favorite, but I liked to reserve that space just in case a song came along that was the actual best song in the world. Anyhow, I wondered if I would ever understand these mysterious changes that were coming for my class or whether I would get left behind. I didn't want to become a reject just because of a bunch of wheat.

And I already missed my parents. Obaachan was so much more strict than my mother or my father. She told us what to eat and drink and how to live. In Japan, her family had a plum tree in their backyard. She was convinced of the healing power of *umeboshi*, Japanese salty plums. They're difficult to eat because they're so sour and salty, but she ate them like candy, spitting the seeds expertly into a bowl. Spitting seeds like that would have gotten me quite a scolding, but as I said, she didn't have to use her manners anymore because she was so old. I didn't like *umeboshi*, so this was a mark against me Japaneseness-wise. Still, I was required to eat two pickled plums a day.

And I had to wear rubber gloves whenever I did the dishes. Even at Obaachan's age, she had beautiful hands. She often held them in front of herself to admire them. The gloves made my hands sweaty, but if she caught me with no gloves on, she would say, "Even if I ugly fish for face, someone would marry me for my hands."

"But you had an arranged marriage," I once pointed out.

"No talk back or I ground you."

I gathered the schoolwork my present and future teachers had given me into a binder. Binders are a great organizational tool. My finished mosquito drawings and the matching original photographs took up one binder. Then I had a binder for all my schoolwork, and another binder to hold new photographs of mosquitoes. Supposedly, I was going to have to spend three hours a day on my schoolwork. Ha-ha. I had already done some of it so that I would have free days. And teachers weren't that strict about work they gave you when you went away on harvest. Once, I had returned from harvest and not done any of my homework, and the teachers barely blinked an eye.

One good thing about harvest is that there are always other kids around who belong to drivers, custom harvesters, or farmers. I had made friends that I'd stayed pen pals with, and even Jaz had made a friend one year, a boy as focused and intense as he was. I was surprised that there could be two such boys in the world. There were probably others as well. I wished they could all meet one another and form a club called the Intense Boys Association.

The night before we left, Jaz was really excited as we lay in bed—he had the bunk above mine. He was hoping he would make a friend during harvest.

"Wouldn't it be great if I make two friends?" he said.

"That would be cool."

"What if I make three? I've never had three friends at the same time before."

Actually, he had never had two friends at the same time either.

He became quiet then, but I knew he wasn't asleep. He was thinking about these three imaginary friends. I hoped he did make three, I really did, but thinking about it made me get a small pain in my stomach, because what was most likely to happen is that he would end up by himself a lot, talking to himself, playing with plastic soldiers, building with LEGOs, and watching movies. If you bothered him while he was playing with his soldiers, he might fly into a rage. You had to wait until he was taking a break.

The hall light went on, and Jiichan came into the bedroom. He pulled up the chair from my desk.

"Tonight I tell you the story of a weed," he said. "One day when I boy, I pulling weeds in orange grove. Day hot, many weed, back hurt. Bad day. Weed came from all over the night before. Suddenly, more weed than I ever see. Weed my special enemy. I hate it more than anything. I have many nightmare about weed. But that day I find special weed I never see before. My mother scold me, but I take weed roots carefully out, and I leave field and put my special weed in jar of water. Then after work I plant it in wet soil. Every day I take care of that weed. It grow as tall as me, and that year we have best-tasting orange crop ever. We raise price because everyone want our oranges. So I want you to remember, always keep eye open for special weed. You both special weed. *Oyasumi*."

"*Oyasuminasai*, Jiichan," we said.

# CHAPTER FOUR

From our home in Littlefield, Kansas, we had to drive across the state to Susanville, Kansas, to meet up with the Parker Harvesting crew. My parents had worked for the Parkers twice, once two years ago and once three years ago. The second time we were short on money, and they paid us for the first month before we'd done any work. That's the kind of people they are.

It was still dark when we set out in our rattly, old Ford pickup. That thing was older than I was. We'd eaten a quick breakfast of oatmeal and two *umeboshi* each. I just pulled on a pair of jeans. I was also slathered in controlled-release

DEET. That was why Thunder didn't lay his head on my lap like he usually did. The company that made the DEET said they used an extra refining process that almost eliminated the smell. I'd grown used to it, but it was apparently too much for Thunder.

Jiichan sort of turned off whenever he drove. He didn't talk much and kept the radio on low. Once in a while he came to life, as if somebody had flipped an "on" switch. As for Jaz, he was blowing giant bubble-gum bubbles, over and over. "Look," he said. "I can blow a bubble the exact same size every time."

On his lap sat a LEGO apartment building he'd been gluing together as he built it. He could have just put it in the truck bed, but he said that it was his most precious possession. End of argument.

Thunder was curled up on the backseat beside me. I opened my window. The air was perfectly lukewarm, but I knew when we got to Texas, that would change. When I checked the Weather Channel before we left, it said it might hit 100 degrees there! Thunder lifted his head and took a big breath, closing his eyes and, I swear, smiling. I stared out the window. The wheat fields were black in the early-morning darkness. I wondered who'd be cutting those. Maybe it would be us as we swung back north.

We drove past mile after mile of wheat, soybean, cattle, and sunflower farms. One of my favorite things was driving through Kansas when both the wild and cultivated sunflowers were in bloom. I liked the wild ones better, the clouds hovering over the tangle of yellow. They would still be in bloom in the fall.

Then I heard Obaachan growling. It was her sign that the pain in her back had become unbearable. Without a word, Jiichan pulled over to the side of the road. He had barely stopped the truck when Obaachan got out and lay flat on her back on the shoulder of the highway. She lay down like that several times a day, sometimes for hours. Jiichan grabbed the flashlight from the glove compartment, and we all stepped outside. Thunder sniffed at Obaachan and then looked at me, as if he knew something about her that he couldn't communicate to us.

We stood around for twenty minutes or so doing nothing but watching. That kind of standing around occurred sometimes in the country, where you were far from medical care. You had to kind of gather around and evaluate. Obaachan looked bad, but I'd seen her worse. She even wore a slight smile, as if she was thinking of something pleasant like me getting all A's or Jaz finding a friend. She had just recently stopped dyeing her hair jet-black, so I could see the white roots like a halo around her face.

Then her smile faded and she said, "We suppose to be there before six."

She reached out her arms without saying anything more, and Jaz and I each took a hand and pulled her up.

Back in the car she said, "I think I die this year, maybe this month."

"I die first," Jiichan replied. "Japanese women live to nineties."

"I die first! You eat many mandarin orange as child. They make you live longer. Vitamin C."

"You drink more green tea. You live longer."

They continued like this for several minutes,

at the end of which I wasn't sure who the matter was settled in favor of. Personally, I planned to live until I was 103, like my great-grandmother on my father's side had. All she did toward the end was watch TV, like it was more important than the real people around her. But there was a lot of good stuff on TV, so it wasn't such a terrible last few years.

We drove quietly, except for Jaz, who popped his perfect bubbles over and over. For some reason, that started to make me crazy. "Can you stop popping your gum so much, please?" I asked him politely.

"Make me."

"You are so immature!"

He gave me a hard, angry look, and then I was already unbuckling my seat belt as he started pounding the side of his head on his window, his LEGO building tottering on his lap. I wrapped my arms around him and squeezed, so he wouldn't hurt himself. I had learned that when you're trying to hold someone still, you had to concentrate on squeezing, just as you had to concentrate when you did math or English. If you tried to do it with just your strength and not your mind, you would fail. In fact, Jiichan taught me to meditate partly because he thought that would help my concentration whenever I had to hold Jaz back.

After a couple of minutes he calmed down. Jiichan had pulled over, and he and Obaachan were watching. Jiichan said sadly, "You lucky to have each other. Why fight?"

"All I did was say he was immature," I said. "Alyssa says that all the time to *her* brother."

"You're not even human!" Jaz cried out. "You're nothing but a smelly DEET bomb! Smellface!"

I set him loose and moved back to look out my window. I wasn't going to talk to him for the rest of the ride. Let's see *him* get malaria and not come out the other end feeling a little paranoid.

"You grounded, Summer," Obaachan said. I didn't answer, but she continued. "You start fight."

I took a big breath. I supposed she was right, but nobody ever thought about how hard it was for me to have Jaz for a brother.

At last we reached the Parkers' house. Jiichan opened the car door, said, "I die first" to Obaachan, and got out, slamming the door.

The sun hung above the horizon, a red ball like on the Japanese flag. That's what the sunrise always made me think of. Uh-oh! The sunrise today was after six! We were late. I hoped we weren't in trouble already.

The Parkers owned a good chunk of land. A whole acre was devoted just to their machines. I saw four combines that I knew they rented; four big rigs (semis) they owned; two camper trailers, one much bigger than the other; a tractor and grain cart; four grain trailers; four pickups; and a variety of trailers to load some of the equipment on. I knew a lot about those machines. The combines were hulking, bright green John Deeres; that's what most harvesters used. The cabs had two seats, and the windows stretched from floor to roof. You drove on the right side instead of the left for some reason.

Combine harvesters are kind of magical machines. This is what happens during harvest: When the wheat is ripe and ready to cut, the combines drive in an orderly fashion, up and down through the wheat fields. In the front of the combine is a detachable apparatus called a header.

The header cuts the crop as the combine moves forward. Then the insides of the combine separate the edible wheat from the inedible chaff and then send the wheat into a bin on the back of the combine. The chaff drops to the ground, where it stays to help fertilize the soil for next year.

I don't know. I mean, maybe computers and cell phones and rocket ships are more magical, but to me, nothing beats the combine. That's just the way I see things. In a short time, the combine takes something humans can't use and then turns it into something that can feed us.

So. The bins hold about 275 bushels of wheat. At the usual speed of five miles per hour, a combine can cut six hundred or so bushels of wheat in an hour. There are a *lot* of variables, and I could be wrong because I'm so bad at math, but, taking some average numbers, six hundred bushels is more than twenty thousand loaves of bread.

To get the wheat grains out of the bin, the combine has an auger, which is a long, hollow, pipelike contraption that pushes the wheat from one end of the auger to the other. The auger moves the wheat from the bin to a grain cart.

A grain cart is attached to a tractor that pulls it up and down the fields. Neither the tractor nor the combine stops moving as the combine driver dumps wheat from the bin to the cart. Not stopping saves time, which is so, so important to harvesting—the grain has to be cut when it's just right.

Stick with me; I'm almost done explaining what happens in the field! The grain cart holds a thousand bushels. When it gets full, the tractor is driven to one of the grain trailers attached to the waiting big rigs, and its auger is used to dump the wheat from the cart into the trailer. When the trailer is full, the big rig takes the wheat to an elevator, where the grain is stored until the farmer sells it.

I learned all this when I was seven and went on my first harvest. You know how there are some people who just love little kids and will take the time to explain anything to them? And then of course there are people who love *their* kids, but pretty much ignore every other kid. Well, that year my parents and grandparents worked for a couple who loved kids—all kids. So they let Jaz

and me ride with anyone we wanted, whenever we wanted. Jaz still talks about that couple sometimes, because they treated him like he was a normal kid, which is kind of unusual. Sometimes I can look into the eyes of a grown-up and see the moment they realize Jaz is different. I still remember that I never saw that in these people's eyes.

Wait, where was I? Oh yeah. So, the grain elevators use systems of augers to move the wheat into the silos. If rain was coming, the process would continue until the early hours of the morning, so that all the farmers could get their wheat in before the rain. Some elevators were even open 24/7.

That's one job I would never want: operating an elevator. Sometimes employees would slip from ladders or walkways and end up suffocating beneath tons of grain. Also, the grain dust in the air could ignite easily. Before I was born, an elevator in Kansas exploded and killed seven people. Another time, six more people died in an elevator explosion. Scary!

Jiichan told me that Mr. and Mrs. Parker had started out as combine drivers, then saved enough to qualify for a loan to buy their first big rig. Now they could afford to hire people like my family to drive the combines and trucks. If you were a custom harvester, you were the boss; but if you were a combine driver, you only worked for a custom harvester and didn't get paid much. My parents hoped to become custom harvesters one day too. They would start out with one semi, or two if the bank would give them a big enough loan.

Like us, the Parkers lived in farm country in a white A-frame house. But their house was a lot bigger.

The front door of the main house was wide open. Thunder sniffed at the doorway. Jiichan tried knocking, but no one answered, so he knocked harder. Obaachan said, "Summer, you call hello. You talk best."

She always said that.

"Hello?" I called out. "Hellloo!" Nobody answered, but we could hear voices from inside. "Let's just go in," I told my grandparents.

"Oh, no," Jiichan said. "Not polite."

"Never go inside if nobody let you in," Obaachan agreed.

"Then we're just going to have to wait here," I

said. "But the door's open. That means we can go inside. I'm sure it's okay."

"No, not okay," Jiichan said, shaking his head.

"Helloooooo!" Jaz suddenly shrieked.

There was an abrupt silence from inside, and then Mr. and Mrs. Parker came to the door. "Toshiro, Yukiko, come in. You don't have to knock!" Mrs. Parker said.

So we took off our shoes and entered. We were wearing running shoes that were identical except for being different sizes. The Parkers' house was pretty inside. A wedding-ring quilt, all in shades of pale blues and yellows and pinks, hung on the wall facing the front door. A quilt was one of two things I had always wanted. The other thing was a wicker chair for the front porch. "What kind of girl wants a wicker chair?" my mother had asked when I'd told her that. I knew why she said that. I mean, the other girls at school coveted smartphones. I would rather have had a wicker chair. Melody thought I was nuts.

I loved the Parkers. They had one son, Robbie, but he was kind of boring. I guess I would play cards with him if I were desperate, but he wasn't interesting like his parents. Mrs. Parker was all business a lot of the time, but she was very kind, and if anyone got hurt, she was all over them like a Band-Aid. She was a large woman with a strong, caring face, the sort of face that made you like her right away because she was nice, but you knew you couldn't take advantage of her.

"Summer, you must have grown three inches," she exclaimed, giving me a hug.

"Yes," I said politely. "I think it's been exactly three inches since you last saw me."

Mrs. Parker's hair was dark reddish, and she had the greenest eyes I'd ever seen. And Mr. Parker reminded me of the president or something—a man who chose to have the weight of the world on him.

"Great, you're here," Mr. Parker said, clapping his hands together once. "We were just talking through our plan for the north part of harvest. Since we have only a thousand acres in South Dakota, we can split up there. Some of us can go on to North Dakota."

I thought it was pretty nice of them not to mention that we were at least half an hour late.

Everyone else was ready to go. It was weird because my grandparents were always saying it was important to be punctual, and they were always rushing around to be on time, but they were almost always late. Sometimes they would start getting ready for something before my parents started, and they would still be late. In fact, the only time I could remember them being on time for anything was for Jaz's meeting-party. They had really wanted that day to be a success.

We followed the Parkers into the kitchen, which was crowded with all the workers they'd hired. In the middle of the room was an island surrounded by stools with green cushions that said JOHN DEERE on them. *John Deere made stools?*

"Lonny, it's a little more than a thousand acres in South Dakota, and there's a chance of finding more," Mrs. Parker gently argued, getting back to the discussion our arrival had interrupted. "So can't we just plan not to have a plan?"

"I guess that's the same plan we have every year," Mr. Parker said, and everybody laughed.

I couldn't wait to get to the Badlands. I'd been there on two different harvesting trips. In the Badlands you could see rocks of every color and shape. One time, over unending cliffs of gray rocks, we saw a cloud-and-fog storm approaching, as if it were aiming right for us. I had never been so scared or so excited. We didn't want to get caught in the fog because then we might have to stay put until we could safely return to our car—What if we walked off a cliff in the fog?

And yet we couldn't leave—it was if the rocks were holding us there. I mean, they were only rocks. But for some reason, those rocks made lonely feel good. Those clouds made you dream big. Not big like you could make a lot of money or like you could have a good job. Bigger than those things. It was complicated. I mean, big like you were part of the sky, which also made you feel small. I don't know how to explain it! The last time I had been there, we'd seen tan rocks shaped like the hides of some sort of animal. Nobody will ever convince me that those rocks weren't as alive as I was. They were just on a different timetable.

"Have some coffee, and then we should get going," Mrs. Parker said to my grandparents. I pulled my mind away from the rocks as Mrs.

Parker began to gesture toward the workers one at a time. "This is Sean Murphy, Rory O'Brien, and Mick Ryan. They're from Ireland. And this is Bill McCoy and Larry Dark. They're American. Folks"—now she was pointing at us—"Toshiro and Yukiko Sakata and their grandkids, Summer and Jaz."

Many custom harvesters hired non-Americans. The Parkers hired their foreign employees legally through an agricultural program at Ohio State University. The employees got paid by the month, regardless of whether they worked sixteen-hour days or hardly any hours because of rain—it was impossible to harvest during a rain because combines can't thresh wheat if it's too moist. Since the hours could be really long, and you had to live for months at a time in a camper, the custom harvesters found that foreign employees were more likely to stick with the job than Americans.

This is how nice the Parkers are: At the end of every season they always take the employees on a special trip, like to a big city or to a NASCAR race. We went to NASCAR with them once, and I have to say that sitting for hours in the sun and watching a bunch of cars speed by me was about the most upside-down day of my life. I mean, everyone—even Jiichan—got all excited when there was an accident right in front of us. If you were a nice person, such as my father and Jiichan and the other workers, why would an accident excite you? It was like all the rules about driving that applied in the outside world didn't apply at NASCAR. Then a bunch of men who worked for NASCAR helped the driver out of his car, and blood dripped down his forhead. He wasn't hurt badly, but still, it was totally bizarre how excited everyone was. My dad said I just didn't understand men and cars, and what they meant to one another, and I said, "Amen to that," and my mom laughed out loud—she *always* says that.

Anyway, the two Americans were older, probably retirement age, like my grandparents. The Irish guys looked like they were in their twenties. Irish workers always used the word "lads," but I thought of them as "guys." "Lads" just didn't sound right. All the men wore jeans and T-shirts with writing or pictures on them. Mr. Dark's shirt said KEEP AMERICA FOR THE AMERICANS, and Rory's said THE NUMBER OF THE BEAST, which was an Iron Maiden record from way back in the early eighties. Some guys at school were obsessed with that music. My grandparents didn't believe in such T-shirts, because why should you pay to advertise for someone else? I had tried to explain to them that you could use T-shirts to express yourself. Jiichan had shaken his head and said woefully, "No can be different by doing same thing as everyone else."

"Will youse two be driving combines, then?" Mick asked. The Irish guys from our last harvest did the same thing—used "ya" for "you" in the singular and "youse" for "you" in the plural. Isn't that cool?

"I drive, she cook," Jiichan said. "She best cook in country."

I tried to figure out who'd be doing what—four semi drivers, three combine drivers, one tractor driver. But that left an extra combine. The logistics always made my head spin. And then there was Obaachan and we three kids (including Robbie). What I *could* figure out is that Obaachan and I would be cooking for twelve every day. Yikes!

48

We all headed outside, and Mr. Parker gave us our driving assignments.

I *think* it went as follows: We'd leave our Ford at the Parkers', and Obaachan would drive one of the Parkers' pickups, which was attached to the smaller camper—the camper the Parkers would be living in. Jaz, Thunder, and I would ride with her. The pickup would also be the service car we would drive for the whole harvest, used to shop for groceries or to make a parts run if any of the machinery broke. Jiichan was driving a semi, which was hauling the tractor and grain cart. The three Irish drivers were each driving a semi, each hauling one combine and one grain trailer for an extra-long load. Mr. Dark and Mr. McCoy would each drive a pickup hauling a combine header. The final vehicle was a pickup, which Mr. Parker would drive hauling a third header. Mrs. Parker and Robbie would ride in that pickup.

We were leaving behind one combine, one grain trailer, the employee camper, and one header . . . I think. I wasn't sure I could keep track of it all at that point. When we reached Texas, the majority of us would start working immediately while three of us would drive back with two semis and a pickup to get the rest of the machinery. By law, the last combine wouldn't be hauled down to Texas until daybreak. Transporting such wide loads was dangerous at night because of overhang into the oncoming traffic.

As everyone made their way to their assigned vehicles, Robbie Parker sauntered out of the house with his hands in his pockets. I had not seen him for two years. He was fourteen now, I thought, and had turned so good-looking that I gaped and was really glad that I'd neatly braided my hair that morning. I only stopped gaping because my grandmother pushed me so hard that I lost my balance.

I helped Obaachan pack some of our essentials in the pickup we'd be driving, but we transferred the rest of our luggage to the employee camper, which would be driven out to us on the second trip. The only special things I brought into the pickup for myself were a spray bottle of DEET and my lifetime savings of $461, which included the special twenty-dollar bill my grandfather had given me when I was five years old. I could still remember him telling me, "Someday this bill may be worth a million dollar. It called inflation."

Once everyone else was packed up and settled in, Mr. Parker pecked Mrs. Parker on the cheek and said, "Let's roll, beautiful."

# CHAPTER FIVE

The air was still cool as we all headed for Hargrove, Texas. I figured it would be about a six-hour drive. I glanced into the side mirror at the line of vehicles behind us.

Obaachan turned onto the highway, then said to me, "Too young to stare at boys."

"I wasn't staring."

"You staring like he alien from outer space. Boys not alien, they real, and they cause trouble."

"How do they cause trouble?"

"You too young to know that." She looked at me as if making a decision. Then she said, "Maybe I tell you if I have time before I die."

"I'm a boy," Jaz said. "I know how they cause trouble."

"You do not," I scoffed at him.

"Stop fight now or I throw you both out of truck and you have to walk to Texas. Jaz, this not involve you," Obaachan said. "Summer, you walk to Texas, you be sorry. I walk twenty mile once when I a girl, and by end I could hardly move. And don't think I forget what we talking about. No stare at Robbie. Everybody notice."

I sighed and gave Thunder's ears a tug. He had natural ears and a docked tail, like a lot of Dobermans today. In some countries it was against the law to crop Dobermans' ears. Personally, I approved of this law. In fact, if someone tried to crop *my* own ears, I would bite them.

"You listen me?" Obaachan said.

"Yes, Obaachan, I heard you."

"Not hear, listen," she shot back.

I looked out the window at a cattle farm. In Kansas agriculture, cattle was number one in terms of how much money it brought the state. Wheat was a distant second. But my whole life had revolved around wheat.

53

"You listen me?" Obaachan asked again.

"Well, how old were you when you started staring at boys?" I asked back.

"That has nothing to do with it."

"But how old were you?" I persisted.

"In my day girl not married by eighteen, she a reject. Different today. Girl get married at thirty. So if I stare at boy at twelve and get married at eighteen, that mean you stare at boy at twenty-four and get married at thirty."

"So you were twelve?" I got more alert—I might finally be about to win an argument with Obaachan.

"I don't say that."

"Then what are you saying?"

"I'm say you make fool of yourself. Give me apple."

I rummaged through the bags on the floor next to me. "There's only pears. I think we left the apples in the camper."

"Don't get smart. Give me pear."

I resignedly gave my grandmother a pear. It was obviously Pick on Summer Day. Once, I asked my mother if Obaachan loved me, and Mom said, "Of

course she does. She thinks about you all the time."
I knew she thought about me all the time, but that
wasn't the same as love, was it? No. It wasn't.

My grandmother ate the pear—seeds, stem,
and all—and then she began emitting that low
growl: "Errrrr."

After a few minutes of this, Jaz asked, "Are we
pulling over?"

"No can," Obaachan said.

"They'll understand," I said.

"They no hire us again. Errrrrrrrr. Errrrrrrrrr."

We had brought seven bottles of painkillers
with us. "Do you want some painkillers?" I asked.

"Six," she replied.

I pulled out a bottle and read the label. "It says
take one, and if that doesn't work, you're allowed
to take another." Plus, I had read in a magazine at
the dentist's office that taking too much over-the-
counter medicine was bad for your liver.

"Give me six."

"Obaachan, that's dangerous."

"I sixty-seven—you young, so you don't
understand yet. Pain more important than death."

I thought that over. I remembered that when

I had malaria, the pain in my joints had made me wish I were dead. Up until then, I'd thought that pain was something that came from the outside, but malaria had taught me to fear pain that came from within. I knew my grandmother's pain came from within. So I handed her the six pills.

She chuckled. "Easy to get my way with you."

I gave her a bottle of water. We had filled plastic bottles with tap water because my grandparents couldn't understand why anyone would pay for something that you could get from your own faucet. Personally, I loved bottled water. It made me feel extravagant and grown-up. When I grew up, I would keep bottles of water in my house at all times. I would have three dogs. My husband would love bottled water and dogs and me. Or maybe I would never be able to afford bottled water, maybe I wouldn't have any dogs, maybe I would never feel extravagant and grown-up, and maybe I would never get married.

"Errrr."

I thought of what Obaachan had said about not stopping the convoy for her. Timing was the essence of harvesting. If we held up the progress of the harvesting team, she was right—We would not get hired again, even if the Parkers liked us as people. When the wheat was ready to harvest, it was ready to harvest *now*, and my grandfather would be working fourteen- or even sixteen-hour days.

Obaachan was squeezing the steering wheel so hard, I thought her beautiful hands might snap.

"Will you be all right?" I asked her.

"It no matter," she replied simply.

And, unfortunately, I knew that was true. I started to think about the next few months. The last time we'd worked for the Parkers, Mrs. Parker had compiled a binder of every meal with every recipe we were to make. For six days a week at breakfast, the drivers ate just milk and cereal. But on Sundays we made a full-on breakfast—pancakes or French toast or omelettes. We made about 250 meals that year. I swear we followed every recipe exactly, but once in a while Mrs. Parker would wrinkle her forehead and say something like, "Maybe you skimped on the sugar?"

"Hey," I said suddenly. "How come Jaz doesn't have a job?"

My grandmother glanced into the rearview mirror. "Summer, you make one more trouble, my head explode and you guilty of murder."

I started to say that heads don't explode, but the radio came to life just then, and Mrs. Parker's voice reported, "It's already eighty-two degrees in Hargrove."

That was nothing. One year in Texas the temperature was 110 when we arrived.

Actually, I was kind of relieved that it was going to be a hot day in Hargrove. The things you feared most during harvest were rain and hail and letting the wheat set too long past its prime. But heat was nothing. Once the wheat was ready to harvest, the weather was the boss. After that came the farmer, and close behind were the custom harvesters. The drivers were below them. The cooks were probably even below that, because the drivers could live without us if they had to. Basically, if either the farmer or the Parkers told one of us to do something, we would do it. And me, I was probably at the very bottom of the heap. So even though the Parkers were nice, we weren't all equals. The Parkers liked to say we were all a family, but that simply wasn't true.

I took out my mosquito notebook and began to leaf through my drawings, even though it was hard to concentrate in the bumpy truck. I was much better at drawing now than I was at the beginning, but I still wasn't very good. My secret goal was to make mosquitoes out of real gold and sell them for jewelry. I had made some big mosquitoes out of clay, but the large size didn't capture their delicacy. It was hard to get the clay thin enough. It always chunked up, and the mosquitoes always looked more like bumblebees. I would have to work on that.

I thought again about how when something almost killed you, you were bonded to it for life. But even during the worst parts of my illness, I knew in my mind that the mosquito hadn't been trying to kill me. That hadn't been its goal. It was just trying to get blood so it could lay eggs—only female mosquitoes bite you.

I stopped at one of my favorite drawings, of a mosquito feeding on nectar amid beautiful flowers. I had started that picture seventeen times before I finally got it right. Almost dying makes you think a lot about death. I remember thinking of my family going on without me, of Jaz growing up and being some kind of rocket scientist with exactly two friends, of my mom crying and crying that I was gone. And now I had this second chance at life. My friends all felt like life would go on forever, but I realized it was something happening *now*. And yet I didn't know what to make of it. "It's because your personality hasn't settled yet," my mother liked to say, as if my personality was dust floating in water.

I went through every page of my mosquito book. When I looked up, Jaz was sifting through some papers the Parkers had given us. In the mirror, I could see that Obaachan's face was pale and worried. She was in a lot of pain.

"We've got twenty-two jobs," Jaz said, holding up one of the papers. The Parkers had given everyone a list of the jobs we'd been assigned. "First one's seven thousand acres."

"I have to pee," I said.

"Look in blue bag," Obaachan replied.

I rummaged through the same bag that held all of Obaachan's painkillers and spotted a glass jar.

"You're kidding, right?" I said.

"No kidding. Don't spill."

Mrs. Parker had pulled us all over a couple of hours earlier at a truck stop, but I didn't have to go then. I had to go now. Jaz turned to me, probably to see if I was really going to use the jar. "Mind your own business," I said. "I decided I don't have to go that bad."

The windows were open, the hot air blowing into our faces. I thought about Robbie and made a mental note to rebraid my hair before we stopped again. It was windy out, the wheat field rippling as we passed. It looked less yellow than usual, more like the color of coffee with a whole lot of milk in it. Jiichan had once told me that he knew someone who knew someone who knew someone who knew a woman who could tell your fortune by looking at the way the wind blew the wheat around you. I would be interested in meeting that woman.

A layer of clouds seemed to be pressing down toward us, more like a ceiling than the sky. Despite those clouds, Texas had mostly been dry this year. When the weather was dry while the wheat was growing, the fields would yield fewer bushels per acre. One harvest in Texas, when there had been a lot of rain, the average yield in the state had been nearly sixty bushels an acre, which was quite a lot. This year it would certainly be less—maybe not even thirty.

"Almost there," Mrs. Parker finally announced over the radio.

I closed the back windows and redid my braids, then sat with sweat dripping down my face. I held up a paper towel to my forehead. "Look what Summer's doing," Jaz said.

"I saw," Obaachan said. "She make *saru* out of herself for boy." *Saru* meant "monkey." I could not wait to be out of that truck.

The convoy turned down a dirt road where a makeshift sign that read PARKERS TURN HERE was stuck on a tree. When we reached the farm, a man was already standing outside motioning us to park. I got out and saw there were water and electrical hookups. That meant we would be staying on the farm in the campers instead of going to an RV park. It was a lot easier when you stayed on the farm, but I missed the RV parks because there were always other harvester kids there.

As soon as the Parkers' camper was hooked up, I was going to use the bathroom in there.

Mr. and Mrs. Parker shook the man's hand. "Mr. Laskey? I'm Lonny Parker. This is my wife, Jenna."

"Nice to meet you," Mr. Laskey said. Mr. Laskey was a tall, balding man, and he looked concerned. "I hope you're ready to hit the ground running. There's rain forecast for next week."

"Absolutely. We brought enough machinery this first trip to start right now."

"Great, great. I want this to be a quick job." He said that with the slightest hint of warning in his voice, like if it wasn't a quick job, he would be irate.

"We'll get your wheat in before then, don't you worry." Mr. Parker studied the fields around him and the low clouds. "Those don't look like rain clouds. Yep, not to worry."

Mr. Laskey nodded. He stood with his arms crossed in front of him, and he looked impatient. I'd discovered that some farmers were very tense people because nearly their whole earnings for the year depended on how their wheat crop turned out during these few days of harvest. All year they prayed for rain, until harvest came and they prayed for no rain. Some of them were real nice, but others were just plain grumps.

But I got it. The wheat couldn't be much more than 13.5 percent moist or the grain elevators wouldn't accept it. Wheat that was too moist could cause fungus. The combines had instruments to measure the wheat's moisture content, and there were handheld gadgets to measure with as well. The Parkers used a moisture meter that looked like a thermos cup. You would fill it with wheat, and it would tell you what the moisture level was.

Grain elevators checked for moisture, weeds, and protein content. Wheat that was too dry would weigh less and thus be worth less. Plus, if you let the wheat ripen too long, the protein content could fall. So timing was everything. Another thing that frightened the farmers was hail. Hail could break the wheat or smash it to the ground. I had actually seen a farmer—a big, burly man—cry during a hailstorm. So farmers just wanted to get the harvest over as soon as possible. As I said, I got it.

Mr. and Mrs. Parker drove the combines down off the trailers they were hauled on. I squinted into the distance and didn't see the end of the wheat field. The house, over to the left, was big. I wondered how many kids the Laskeys had and whether we would meet them.

Jiichan steered the tractor and grain cart off the trailer. Then the Parkers had to attach the headers to the front of the combines. The headers, as I mentioned, were the rotating parts of the combines that actually cut the wheat.

John Deere support trucks always followed the harvest because different custom harvesting companies would all be in about the same part of the country at the same time. The support trucks were full of combine parts and manned with John Deere mechanics who could come and help you with your combine if there was a problem. Usually, you didn't need an expert because most harvest crews had a good mechanic on hand. In our case, the best mechanic was Mr. Parker. But if something electrical broke down, you needed a John Deere guy.

I watched Mr. Dark and Mr. McCoy get into two semis and Mr. Parker into a pickup. They roared off back to Kansas to get the rest of the machinery. Poor guys—they'd be driving practically eighteen hours by the time they were done. Then two of the combines and the grain cart headed for the field. It all sounded like an airplane taking off.

When the noise subsided, Mrs. Parker, looking worried, approached us. "You should probably find a grocery store right away, so you can make the crew sandwiches." She handed a stack of binders to Obaachan. "I've planned out the meals for the entire season, complete with recipes, like always. It took me a long time, so please follow the meal plans to a T." She started to walk away, then turned around again. "Why don't you make them tuna sandwiches for lunch? Just remember that my husband isn't fond of too much mayonnaise. He likes mayonnaise, but not too much of it." She gave a little laugh. "Of course, he won't be having lunch today since he left, but I'm reminding you for the future."

She stood for a moment, frowning some more. "On second thought, why don't you make chicken salad sandwiches? I have tuna casserole on the menu for next week, so we don't want to bombard everyone with tuna, and I have tuna again for sandwiches on day twelve." She still couldn't bring herself to turn around and leave. "Always use wheat bread. I don't know why they still manufacture white bread. . . ." Her voice trailed off. She bit at a thumbnail. "And get ice for the cooler, since the refrigerators are in the other camper. You can put any extra food in the cooler—it's a big one. Get enough to make sandwiches for dinner, too." She handed just two twenties to Obaachan.

"She has a photographic memory," said a voice behind me. I turned around and found myself face-to-face with Robbie. OMG. He was talking not to Obaachan but to me. "She has the menus for the entire season in her head. I think we should save her brain when she dies to compare it to Einstein's."

"Wow," I said. That wasn't the most brilliant thing to say, so I added, "That's amazing." That still didn't seem very brilliant, so I came up with, "I mean, it's really cool. Einstein." That was the best I could do for now.

"Robbie doesn't like it because I never forget a thing," Mrs. Parker said with a laugh. "Isn't that true, hon?" She looked at him with what could only be called overwhelming love.

"It makes you hard to argue with," he said. But he smiled, and she smiled. I could probably count on two hands the times Obaachan and I had smiled at each other, and those times only happened when we were watching her favorite TV show, *America's Funniest Home Videos*. I think watching people fall down and barrel into trees was her most favorite thing to do in the world.

Mrs. Parker and Robbie walked off together to the combine she was driving. Mr. Laskey headed toward his house. There was nobody left to tell us where a grocery store might be.

# CHAPTER SIX

After I went to the bathroom and Obaachan's aspirin kicked in, she, Jaz, Thunder, and I got back into the pickup. Obaachan made a slow, wide U-turn, and once again we were bumping along the dirt road. "Which way should we head?" I asked. "I didn't see a store on the highway."

"Errrr."

If I'd been with my parents, I knew I wouldn't have to participate in finding a store. They would take care of it. But with Obaachan, who could say what would happen? Then out of nowhere the thought popped into my head: *I should have used the word "impressive," as in "It's really impressive that your mother has a photographic memory.*" I made a mental note to say that to Robbie some other time.

"Is there map in glove compartment?" Obaachan asked. Jaz began going through the glove compartment. He turned over each slip of paper and read it for a moment, as if that were the only way to determine if it was a map.

"Just a map of the whole country," he finally said.

Obaachan drove to the highway and kept going until we got to a gas station. Then she pulled up and turned to me. "Go ask where grocery store is, Miss Talk So Good."

I got out and walked into the station. There were a few candy bars and drinks for sale, but there was no mini-mart like in many gas stations. The attendant was sitting on a stool behind the counter. "Hi," I said.

"Hello, young lady."

"Can you tell me where the closest grocery store is?"

"What are you looking for?"

I paused. "A grocery store," I repeated.

"I mean, what do you need to buy?"

71

"Bread, canned chicken, lettuce, tomatoes, and mayonnaise."

"Sounds like you want to make a sandwich." He lazily spun his stool around until he was facing me again.

"Yes, sandwiches."

The man asked, "Do you need any drinks to go with those sandwiches?"

"Yes, drinks."

He gestured grandly to where the drinks were in a small refrigerator.

I hesitated before turning and walking out and up to the driver's-seat window. "He wants to know if I need to buy any drinks. They have Coke and stuff."

"He tell you where grocery store is?" Obaachan asked.

"No, I think he wants me to buy drinks."

"How much drinks cost in there?"

"I didn't ask."

Obaachan looked worried. "What if drinks here too expensive and we no have enough money for food? Get in seat." She restarted the engine as I got in.

72

We drove to a small restaurant, but it was closed, maybe forever. It wasn't boarded up, but it just had that aura of something that was closed forever. Farther down the highway, more glass windows in what used to be stores were boarded up. I remembered learning in school that some small towns in the Great Plains were closing up as children grew older and moved to the cities.

We drove all the way to the grain elevator about ten miles away.

"I go this time," Obaachan said. She got out and was gone for what seemed like hours. I started timing her after a while. Thirty minutes passed. The sweat dripped down my forehead, getting DEET into my eyes. They instantly started tearing up, the sting was so bad.

"I think you should go in," Jaz finally said.

"No, here she comes."

Obaachan got into the truck with a paper in her hand.

"What took you so long?" I asked.

"We talk about wheat and Japanese woman his second cousin marry." She started the engine.

"What does she have to do with wheat?"

"Nothing. He want to talk about it after he see me. I talk to him because he give good direction." She pulled onto the highway again. "Big store in next town, but smaller one nearby. Keep eye open for Carver Avenue."

We drove about a mile before we spotted Carver. Obaachan turned right, and we drove and drove and drove until she finally pulled over. She handed me the directions. "Read this. What I do wrong?"

I looked at the lines scrawled on the paper. "We were supposed to turn left on Carver."

"He tell me right and draw left on map. I may not have photograph memory, but I know I right about this."

When we finally reached the store, more than an hour had passed since we'd left the Laskey place. I had a sinking feeling that this was probably what the whole summer would be like as we searched for groceries in each new town, with me, Miss Talk So Good, asking clerk after clerk where the grocery store was. But it didn't bother me so much. I knew we were here to save the mortgage.

By the time we got back to the farm, it was close to two thirty. Obaachan's back was killing her. Still, she laid out a plastic cloth we'd bought with our own money and made the sandwiches on that. Obaachan was a perfectionist. Her sandwiches were works of art. She cut them into perfectly symmetrical triangles and always added a slice of onion so thin, you hardly knew it was there. And the meat was always in just the right place. You'd never take a bite and get too much bread and not enough meat. Then she'd use parsley to make it fancy, except she tore off parts of the parsley so that it looked more like a little flourish. I'd actually helped her write an article about sandwich making. She sent the article to a local paper,

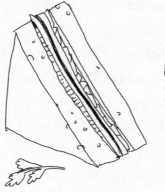

and when they didn't publish it, she canceled our subscription.

The crew was probably starving to death. "You tell Mrs. Parker I finish. Don't say 'we' finish," she told me.

I climbed into the pickup and pressed the button on the radio. Mrs. Parker was still out driving one of the combines. "My grandmother is finished making the sandwiches," I told her. "She'll be right there."

Obaachan had climbed into the driver's seat with the sandwiches.

"What on Earth took so long?" Mrs. Parker asked.

"We had to find the store," I said politely.

There was no answer at first, and then she said, "All right." She clicked off, then clicked on again. "I forgot to tell you about the timetable. Starting tomorrow, we need breakfast at seven, lunch at noon, and dinner at seven. Why did it take so long to find a store?"

"We were unfamiliar with the area," I answered.

"Couldn't you ask someone?"

Obaachan yanked the microphone out of my

hand and said, "Man at elevator where we get direction have to talk to me before he give me direction! It not my choice. You need talk to him."

"What did he have to talk to you about?"

"His second cousin wife."

No one said more into the radio.

"Mrs. Parker already drive me crazy," Obaachan said. But I figured that before long, Obaachan would be driving Mrs. Parker crazy, so it would be even Steven.

Just for something to do, Jaz, Thunder, and I drove into the field with Obaachan.

Robbie was busy with what appeared to be a handheld video game or maybe a smartphone. Jaz would probably have sold me for a quarter if it meant he could get a video game. I thought about yelling hi to Robbie, but why couldn't he be the one to call out to me? So neither of us said anything to the other, and after we gave Mrs. Parker the sandwiches, the combine roared away, Robbie disappearing into the fields.

When we got back, Obaachan groaned. "My neck is kill me, so you make dinner later. I may get up to help. Errrrrr." She lay down on the ground, right where she'd been standing, in the shade from the pickup. First she dropped to all fours, and then she lowered herself carefully to her back.

I sat in the shade beside her and opened my sketchbook to a half-finished picture of a mosquito hanging in the air near a leaf. I had to draw his leg over and over before I could get it right. It was a male. A male mosquito has featherlike antennae that are fun to draw. The antennae of the female are more simple, and the palps are short. Palps help mosquitoes taste. Then there's the evil proboscis. It's like a living spear that stretches out

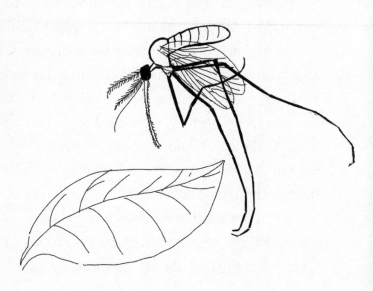

from around a mosquito's mouth. The females use it to stick in you and suck your blood and sometimes kill you. I had memorized this from Wikipedia: "Death is the permanent termination of the biological functions that sustain a living organism."

Once, I had a very old dog, Shika, who one day followed me to the washing machine. I stopped to pet her, and I could sense that she really, really, really wanted to be petted. Then I pulled a comforter out of the washer and put it in the dryer. When I turned around, my dog was lying dead. I lay on the ground beside her and just held her until my mother found us. I didn't even know how much time had passed, but the dryer had stopped. She'd known she was about to die and that was why she'd been so open to being petted.

My mother said that when I was dying and the nurse had left the room, Obaachan had lain beside me on the bed and held me. That was so hard for me to believe I thought my mother might be lying.

After I finished with my mosquito sketchbook, I picked up one of the books I had to read for school.

It was called *A Separate Peace*. My teacher said I had to read three books over the summer. Even though it was for older kids, I chose *A Separate Peace* because it was the only book in English that Jiichan had ever read, and he wanted me to explain it to him. He was very troubled by the book and had been after me to read it all year. It was about two Caucasian guys who went to a boarding school during World War II. In other words, it was about a world completely alien to mine. I was already on page 30. Some kids I knew would read only books that were about something they could relate to. But I was interested in other stuff.

Jaz, in a huge straw hat, worked on his LEGO building right out in the hot sun. He was concentrating so hard on the building that I don't know if he even realized he was in the sun. His construction was really very impressive. There were four floors, with balconies, and the insides were furnished. Nobody could talk to him when he was focused on his LEGOs, because he might have a meltdown. He might pound his head on something. He might throw a cup at you.

I looked around at the wheat in the distance.

I knew there was also wheat on the other side of the highway. There was nowhere to go except to other wheat fields and nothing to do except walk through the wheat fields.

All three of us were drenched with sweat. I wished they had brought the employee camper first, but I also understood that working the fields was more important than whether or not I was sweating. I read the last few chapters of *A Separate Peace*. Okay, that wasn't a good move. Now I felt even more confused. So I went back to where I was before to keep reading from there.

Later, as I took the chicken out of the cooler to prepare sandwiches for dinner, I suddenly realized I was thinking about *A Separate Peace*, just like Jiichan. The book made me think about what was deep inside of me. Was I good or bad or mixed or what? And was the way I acted every day the real me, or was the real me somewhere so deep that I would never even know it? I made a mental note to talk about this with Melody when I got back home. Then I tried to remember, *Wasn't there another mental note I made to myself earlier?* I couldn't remember. Maybe I needed to start writing down my mental notes. Who knows what all I'd forgotten to do over the years? But then what if someone got ahold of my notebook and some of the mental notes were embarrassing?

Back to *A Separate Peace*. Why would a book in which hardly anything happened for most of the time eat at me so much? It was the weirdest thing.

The radio crackled to life. It was Mrs. Parker. "If you can hear me, can you cut the sandwiches into rectangles, not triangles? It makes them easier to eat."

"I going to cut her into rectangles," murmured Obaachan.

I hopped into the truck and picked up the radio. "Hi, it's Summer. We'll definitely cut into rectangles this time. I think my grandmother thinks triangles look better."

"I don't mean to micromanage," said Mrs. Parker, "but could you and/or she also use just a touch more mayonnaise? I think even my husband would have liked a bit more if he were here."

"Okay." I waited, but she didn't say anything further.

"Actually, I want less mayonnaise on mine," Jaz said. "And as long as we're bossing you around, can you slice my tomato really thin? I like some tomato, but not too thick."

"I like thick tomato," Obaachan said.

I wished I had an MP3 player so I could drown everybody out. We'd bought a cheap knife at the grocery store, and when I tried to cut Jaz's tomato thin, I ended up squishing the tomato.

"And don't give me the end part of the tomato with all the skin," Jaz said. "Even if it's thin, I don't want that part."

If Obaachan weren't right there, I would have told him to shut up. Then I did say it: "Shut up!"

I waited for Obaachan to say something, but at first she didn't. Finally, she said, "You grounded, Summer. Errrr."

How could I be grounded on harvest?

"You too sensitive. You need to be tough cookie."

Actually, harvest was a good time to make trouble, because I *couldn't* get grounded. I made a mental note to test out that theory. Then I sighed and carefully cut a thin slice of tomato. I made the sandwiches with a little bit more mayonnaise, except for Jaz's sandwich. I gave everyone except Jaz a thick slice of tomato. And I cut all the sandwiches in half, into rectangles. The problem with me, I decided, was that I was too good. I mean, every so often I was bad, but nobody took me seriously enough. Like, Jaz had everybody in the palm of his hand because of his temper. Everyone took his temper seriously. If I threw a cup across a room like Jaz sometimes did, my entire family would have a nervous breakdown. But maybe that wasn't a bad thing if it made them take me more seriously.

The radio came to life again. "Are the sandwiches ready?"

I grabbed the radio. "Yes, they're ready," I said.

We drove out to the combines, and Mrs. Parker couldn't stop herself from examining the sandwiches before she distributed them.

She suddenly ran her hand over my head and said, "How are you holding up, dear?"

"I'm reading and drawing, and Jaz is playing with his LEGOs."

"Don't worry, it won't be this bad every time."

Then she gave a laugh. "Well, I can't promise you that. One thing about harvest is that anything can happen."

I smiled. "Remember that time I fell off the combine and everyone thought I had a concussion?"

She laughed again. "Honey, some of us just aren't blessed with coordination."

I couldn't stand Robbie just sitting up there, so I said, "How's Robbie doing?"

"He's obsessed with Angry Birds. I have to hide his phone every night so he doesn't stay up playing."

I looked up longingly at him, then quickly looked away so Mrs. Parker wouldn't notice.

After that I really had nothing to do, especially since it would be dark soon. We didn't have any artificial lights, so at least there wouldn't be so many insects around. Just the usual crickets. They were chirping up a storm because of the high temperature—they chirp faster the higher the temperature.

If all went well, the semi with the employee camper would probably be back by one a.m., maybe around the same time that the combines would finish. I found a pen and a piece of scratch paper in the glove compartment of the truck and turned on the inside light. Let's see. On a perfect day, four combines together might cut eighty acres per hour. Eighty times sixteen hours of work equals 1,280 acres a day. So since the farm was about seven thousand acres, and since nothing ever went perfectly, it would take at least seven days to finish the job.

GRAIN CART + BIG-RIG TRAILERS = <u>1,000 BUSHELS EACH</u>

COMBINE: <u>275 BUSHELS</u>

@ 5 MPH    1 COMBINE CUTS 15-20 ACRES PER HOUR
× 20-60 BUSHELS
──────────────────
300-1200 BUSHELS PER HOUR

DEPENDING ON CONDITIONS

So you already know that the grain cart dumps into the grain trailers, and the big rigs take the full trailers to the elevators. Sometimes the wait at the elevators is as long as five or six hours; other times nobody at all will be in front of you. The nearest elevator, the one Obaachan stopped at, was going to stay open until around ten p.m., she'd found out. Some custom harvesters try to have the combine bins and grain trailers empty around elevator closing time. Then everyone would keep working for a few hours more until all the containers were full again. Only then, at one or two a.m., did the work stop. That way, early in the morning, when the elevators opened, the big rigs could go straight to the elevators to dump. The Parkers didn't like to work their drivers past midnight unless it was necessary to beat the weather. And why was I thinking about this stuff? *I* was done for the day and couldn't wait for our camper to arrive so we could all go to sleep in style. But I wondered if Jiichan was getting tired out there.

I got out again and walked around with Thunder. I heard buzzing in my ear—a mosquito! I screamed and shook myself like crazy. Jaz always

87

said that when I shook myself, I looked like a zombie on fire. It was only a myth that just female mosquitoes buzz. Both male and female mosquitoes buzz. Thunder barked, but I wasn't sure what he was barking at. I loved being in my bare feet. So I took off my shoes, which my mother always warned me not to do, because apparently, you could step on all sorts of terrible things outside— to her, the ground was a battlefield.

It was pitch-black, which made it kind of exciting. Thunder and I walked slowly so as not to walk into anything. It was daytime in Japan right now, and my mother was probably helping out with my great-grandparents, washing them or feeding them or just keeping them company.

I stopped and stared straight ahead into the darkness. I felt like I was part of the darkness, in a good way. Sometimes I loved farm life, the way you felt like you were such a part of the dirt and the wheat and the trees and the grass.

I heard something moving, and my heart began to thud. It was probably a coyote, and Thunder would scare it away. Still, now that I was scared, I didn't want to walk anymore. Jiichan said that since I'd gotten sick, I'd turned into a scaredy-cat. Well, things moving in the dark *were* scary! I turned around and hoped I was going in the right direction. I couldn't even see any lights from the combines. They must have been on the far end of the field.

I called out, "Jaz?" He didn't answer, so I called louder, "Jaz?"

Obaachan shouted back, "You bother everybody with your noise! You walk loud like rhinoceros in jungle!"

I seriously doubted that she had ever heard a rhinoceros walk in the jungle, but I was glad to hear her voice. I walked toward it. In a few minutes Obaachan said, "Over here."

I held out my hands and moved them back and forth until I felt the pickup. I stepped on Obaachan's hand by accident and she cried out, "My hand! You ruin my perfect hand!"

"I'm sorry! Where's Jaz?"

"He sleep in truck. You go too."

I climbed into the pickup with Thunder and lay down on the backseat. Thunder tried crawling on top of me. I couldn't push him off, though, because he was too strong and stubborn. So I lay there with ninety-five pounds of Doberman on top of me. Seriously, Dobermans have elbows like rocks. I concentrated all my energy, the way I did when I was holding Jaz, and with a grunt, I pushed off Thunder. He curled up on the floor and went to sleep.

I woke up to a commotion. A big rig had arrived with the employee camper. Jaz was sitting up, stretching on the front seat. The back doors of the pickup couldn't open unless a front door was open, so I climbed over the front seat and got out with Thunder and Jaz. Mr. Laskey had apparently woken up with the noise as well and was standing nearby in a robe. The other combines were in from the field. I squinted at the headlights of the big rigs, then checked my watch: 2:47 a.m.

Mr. Parker was already attaching the employee camper to the water and electricity hookups. Yay—a real bed! I staggered into the camper and felt for the light along the wall. I turned it on and found myself standing in the kitchen. To the right of that was a couch and TV. Then

I checked out both ends of the camper, which turned out to be identical. Each had six beds—two three-level bunks. I knew my grandparents would want the bottom bunks. I took a middle bunk so that Thunder would be able to get up into it. I told him "Hup!" and he struggled onto the narrow bed.

Even though the bed was hard, it felt really comfortable compared to the backseat of the pickup. I usually liked to take a shower before bed, but I was so tired, I thought I'd be able to fall asleep without being clean. The rest of my family trudged in together. Jiichan looked exhausted; the lines on his face seemed deeper than usual, as if he were a lifetime smoker. "You want air conditioner, Toshi?" Obaachan asked.

"*Hai,*" he said, lying down with a grunt.

"I'll get it," Jaz said. He turned it on and climbed to the top of the other bunk. I could tell how tired he was by how he kind of slapped his hands onto the rungs instead of grabbing them firmly.

Obaachan eyed her bed critically, then pushed at it a couple of times with her hand. "Summer, pull mattress off for me. I sleep with it on floor."

I climbed down obediently, pulled off the mattress, and climbed back up.

"I change my mind," she said. "I think I sleep with mattress on bed. Summer."

I had a feeling she was doing this on purpose, but what could I do? I climbed down and put the mattress back on the bed. This time I waited. "Well?" I asked.

"Floor is better."

"That's what I figured."

"You smart-mouth me?"

"No, it's just what I figured, that's all." She looked at me suspiciously, but I just pulled the mattress to the floor without another word. Then I turned out the light and got in bed.

"Ah, *kita makura*!" Obaachan said. She groaned and I heard rummaging before she groaned again.

*Kita makura* was the Japanese superstition that sleeping with your head to the north was bad luck. The beds had already been made, with the pillows on the north. I supposed Obaachan had just moved around so that her head was now facing south. But then she said, "Summer."

"Yes?"

"I want to sleep east. Change my mattress. It too heavy for me."

In fact, it wasn't heavy at all, but I climbed down carefully and felt my way to the light switch. I didn't know how I was going to survive the whole summer without killing somebody.

"Never mind," she said. "I like south after all."

"You're doing this on purpose!" I cried out.

"What you mean?" She gave me her best innocent look. That made me even more suspicious.

"You're making me climb up and down just because you think it's funny!"

"What funny about that?"

"Well, do you want anything else before I get back in bed?" I asked, exasperated.

"What would I want? It middle of night."

Obaachan lay down and closed her eyes. By the time I got back in bed, I was wide awake. I stared into the blackness and thought about practice-kissing my hand and pretending it was Robbie. But somehow Obaachan would probably know, and I didn't want to be humiliated. I turned on my side, my back to the rest of the room, and gave my hand a little peck. I wasn't sure how stiff to keep my lips. I wasn't sure how much to move my lips. None of my friends had ever kissed a boy, but another girl in class had kissed a boy at a party, and after she did it, the boy passed her a note in class calling her the Rock of Gibraltar because he said her lips were so hard. She had cried in class, right in the middle of math. Something like that could pretty much ruin your whole life.

# CHAPTER SEVEN

When I opened my eyes the next morning, Obaachan wasn't on her mattress. Jaz and Jiichan were still sleeping. I climbed down—Thunder jumped—and padded toward the kitchen area. I stopped when I saw that the Irish guys, Mr. McCoy, and the Parkers were already eating cereal, all squeezed together on the built-in benches. Mr. Dark was probably on the road from Kansas, hauling the fourth combine. Then Obaachan spotted me and said, "Summer, you eat cereal. Hurry, before it all gone." I walked into the room feeling thoroughly embarrassed to be seen by Robbie in one of the stupid T-shirts I always slept in. Across the front it said I LOVE HOUSEWORK—NOT.

"I love housework—not," Robbie read in a monotone.

"Ah, ya'll make someone a fine wife one day," Mick said, and everybody laughed.

I was trapped. I snatched up a box of Cap'n Crunch and poured it into a bowl, adding just a little milk, since there wasn't much left. Obaachan shook her head at me for some reason. I held the bowl in one hand and the spoon in the other.

"Oh, sit down, dear," said Mrs. Parker. "There, squeeze in next to Robbie."

Everybody squished together even more, and I sat next to Robbie, our shoulders pressing against each other. Even though my T-shirt already reached almost to my knees, I stretched it down as much as I could.

"It's the strangest thing—your face is flaming red," Mrs. Parker said. "Do you have a fever?"

Everybody looked at me. "I'm fine," I said. I faked a smile and spooned cereal into my mouth.

Mrs. Parker laughed. "I think you have the messiest hair I've ever seen."

"Yes, ma'am, it gets very tangled at night," I

said. "I thrash." Could this possibly get any more embarrassing?

"Goodness, maybe you should cut it."

"Yes, maybe."

And yes, it *could* get more embarrassing. Because then Robbie said, "You smell funny. Like . . . insecticide?"

"Robbie has a very good nose," Mrs. Parker said.

Great. "Last year I actually almost died from malaria that I caught in Florida, so I use DEET. It gets on my clothes."

He looked at me thoughtfully, as if I had just said something profound. One of his green eyes held a tiny spot of hazel. He was the most beautiful person I had ever seen. Then suddenly he looked mischievous. "You heard of washing machines?" he asked, almost tauntingly.

I paused. I thought about something smart to say, something that would un-embarrass myself. Then I said, "We don't have a washing machine at home. We put soap and water in the bathtub, and I stomp on our laundry."

Robbie paused. Then, since I was only kidding, I smiled slyly, and he smiled back.

97

"You're kidding. You're okay," he said, then poured some more cereal.

Yeah! No matter what else happened, the entire day was now a success because I was okay!

I finished my Cap'n Crunch while everybody talked about harvest. If everything went well, we would be heading for Oklahoma in about a week. Rain was coming, but during growing season, Texas had been in a drought, so there wasn't much business here. Some harvesters weren't even bothering to come down to Texas. According to Mr. Parker, to get to Oklahoma in time meant sixteen-hour days every day. Farmers—and custom harvesters—weren't happy until every single grain was in the elevator. Only then could anyone relax.

Robbie checked his watch, as if he had an appointment, and turned to me. "Did you bring a lot of schoolwork?"

"Yeah, but I probably won't do all of it. The teachers really don't expect harvesting kids to do all their homework."

"I know, but I gotta do all mine, anyway. My dad's a tyrant. Are you gonna help your grandmother cook?"

"Uh-huh. That's my biggest chore. I have to help with every single meal. Washing the dishes, boiling turkey, whatever. Do you have chores?"

"Like I said, my dad's a tyrant. So almost every time we change farms, I have to clean and check the combines. I check all the fluid levels—the engine oil, the water, the hydraulic oil. I check the tires. Then I look over the sickle sections and guards. Then I grease all the ten-hour zerks. There are also twenty-five-, fifty-, and hundred-hour zerks, but they need to be greased only after the machine runs that many hours. I blow out the filters. And I have to wash the windows and clean the inside of the cabs."

"That sounds like a lot of stuff," I said. I knew only a bit about cleaning combines, because once when I couldn't sleep on harvest, I went outside and found my dad cleaning his combine. Many custom harvesters made each employee clean his or her own combine. We were lucky to have an extra person—namely, Robbie—to help us.

"It takes about an hour per combine." He shrugged. "I like it. I'd better like it, because I'm going to be doing it until I go to college."

"Wow," I said. He had three little freckles right above his lips.

"Wow what?"

"Wow, I never even think about college."

"How old are you again?" he asked.

"I'm twelve, but I'm really thirteen because that'll be my next age." That made no sense, but Robbie didn't say anything.

There was a knock on the door, and then it opened before anyone had a chance to say "come in." It was Mr. Laskey. "Has anybody checked the moisture level yet? We had a pretty dry night. Might be time to cut already," he said.

"I checked thirty minutes ago and it was fourteen-point-five," Mr. Parker told him.

"Then it might be ready now."

Though he wasn't finished eating, Mr. Parker got right up and went outside with Mr. Laskey.

Everybody followed except for Obaachan and me. It didn't change my life if the wheat was ready to cut or not. I started clearing off the table.

It was pretty easy because, like I said, in the menu books, Sundays were the only days when we made a full breakfast, with scrambled eggs and sausage and toast and stuff. I loved *iri tamago*—eggs scrambled with sugar and *shoyu* and rice wine. It sounded so weird when people called *shoyu* "soy sauce." It made it sound like Tabasco or something instead of the clean and perfect thing that it was. Anyway, I made a mental note to ask Mrs. Parker if we could make that for everybody one Sunday.

Obaachan picked up a bowl I'd put in the rack. "What this?" she asked, pointing at it.

I had to admit there was a little piece of gunk stuck to the outside of the bowl. I took the bowl back and rewashed it while Obaachan checked and then dried every dish in the rack.

"I clean counters, you walk Thunder, then do homework."

I got a tennis ball and walked out with Thunder into the bright sunshine. I threw the ball for him for about fifteen minutes, until his tongue was hanging long out of his mouth. I got him some water, hoping he'd perk up and play longer, so I wouldn't have to do homework yet, but he just lapped up the whole bowl and went to the camper door and looked at me. Okay, then. Homework time for me.

Inside, Jaz was at the kitchen table doing his so-called homework. He was supposed to be making a detailed family tree, but I knew he was making up some of it. Our family consisted of farmers and fishermen as far back as anyone knew, but when I'd sneaked a peek at his paper earlier, he'd claimed we had several samurai in our background.

I took down *A Separate Peace* and finished reading the middle part. So I'd read the first part first, the last part second, and the middle part third. I didn't know how I would write my book report, because I just plain didn't understand the book. Next I read the parts I hadn't read. The book was supposed to be for high schoolers, but a sister of one of my friends was in high school, and she thought it was the worst book she ever read. And even though I kind of agreed with her, I also kind of disagreed with her. Maybe I should just write the truth and say that it was the worst book I ever read, but that it made me wonder things about myself. It made me think that each person had all sorts of things going on inside of them, but most of these things would never surface unless circumstances were exactly right. So basically, inside of me was a big wilderness, and then around the wilderness was a nice, mowed lawn. After I thought that, I admit I figured I was kind of a genius. The only problem was that I had taken an IQ test once, so I knew I wasn't a genius.

Jiichan had wanted Jaz and me to take the test so he could understand us better. Jaz scored "very superior," but when it came to real life, he basically flunked. I ended up with an overall score called "high average." But what I didn't understand was, did that mean I always operated on "high average," or did that mean sometimes I operated on "very superior" and other times on "low average"? On the other hand, whatever.

I hugged Thunder to me. Once, Jaz told a boy in my class that I still slept with a stuffed penguin, and so I told Jaz that I loved Thunder ten times more than I loved him. I got grounded for a week by my mother. Her big concern was that my love for Thunder might stunt my "socialization," as she called it. How could I be unsocialized when I had so many friends? If I put together all the times I had ever been grounded, I wondered how much time that would be. Three months? Five? Eight?

After Obaachan had cleaned the table and counters, she lay on her back in the kitchen area. After a while she pushed herself up with a grunt and said, "We go to supermarket now. Mrs. Parker like fresh meat, not frozen. And we need fruit and vegetable."

Jaz and I stood up. "Can I read what you wrote?" I asked him.

"No, it's none of your business."

"But your family tree should be exactly the same as my family tree."

"Then what do you need to read it for?" he asked.

We all got into the pickup—Thunder too—and headed for town.

We drove down the dirt road to the highway. "I wonder which way supermarket," Obaachan said. "Summer, you pick, and if you wrong, you make lunch by yourself all week."

"Why didn't you ask someone?" I asked.

"Because nobody's as smart as you," Jaz said.

"I'm not going to pick," I protested.

Obaachan nodded her head a few times and turned left. We drove down the highway, surrounded by wheat fields. You just couldn't get away from them.

Out of the blue Obaachan said, "Fifteen times four."

She liked to test my math because I wasn't very good at it. Of course, we were way past multiplication tables in school. "Sixty," I said.

"No!"

"Obaachan, it is."

She pulled the truck over and took out a pen and paper from her handbag. "Let's see . . . carry two . . . Okay, you right. See? You say I never admit when I wrong. Take that back."

"But this is the first time."

"Take back and say you make mistake."

"I take it back and I made a mistake," I said. I didn't see how she could turn her being wrong into me saying I made a mistake. So I added, "But you made a mistake too!"

"That subject finished," she replied.

Jaz hit his head softly on the dashboard. With each thunk, he'd say one word. "I. Didn't. Make. A. Mistake."

Basically, Thunder was the only normal person

in the truck, and he wasn't even a person.

Jaz suddenly sat very straight and still, and then his shoulders relaxed again. Then he started talking.

"So last night I woke up and my action figures were alive. They were talking about a raging battle. The sergeant asked me if I wanted to go fight, but I didn't want to because I was too sleepy."

I looked out the window as Jaz's voice continued. "The sergeant told me to take a cold shower to wake myself up. So I did that, but then I thought I still didn't want to go to battle because I'm just a kid. Battles are for grown-ups."

I leaned back as he went on, talking about what each action figure was wearing, what their dog tag numbers were, what their hair looked like, if they had skinny or fat fingers, and a million other details. My parents had taken him to three different child psychologists in Wichita. One psychologist said he had ADHD, one said he had PDD-NOS, and one said he was OCD. I wasn't sure what the initials stood for except for OCD, which meant "obsessive-compulsive disorder." That was why he would use only his three special cups. All three doctors wanted him on medication for his head-banging, but my parents refused. So did my grandparents. We had all learned to live with him, so what was the problem? It was just a part of life.

Though nothing was in front of us, Obaachan suddenly slowed down, and we all jerked forward with the momentum. My grandmother's braking strategy was always a mystery to me. I was about to ask her why she'd braked but then thought better of it, because she would only say something that would somehow make it all *my* fault. I might not have been a genius in general, but when it came to Obaachan, I did have a smart thought now and then.

I leaned over Thunder and made little noises like most people would for a baby. Obaachan kept up her strange braking strategy. Finally, I couldn't stop myself. "Obaachan, why do you keep braking?" I asked.

"Every time you make noise to Thunder, I think I about to hit something. It your fault. If you no like, call taxi."

I ignored that.

There was no wind, and the wheat was still.

I wondered what the fortune-teller would say about that. The sky filled suddenly with clouds, but they disappeared so quickly that you would have had a hard time convincing someone it had just been cloudy.

I peered through the back windshield at the highway curving through the wheat. Highway. Wheat. Sky. So simple. Compared to a city like Wichita, it all looked like a doorway to another world—our world. I always had this weird feeling as I stared out at the wheat, like the dust of my personality was settling a bit, like instead of me ever being confused or with my thoughts all over the place, I was just me, without any questions about anything or any worries or even any sadness. But that was impossible, because I didn't even like wheat. Did I?

A mosquito zzz-ed in the air in front of me, and I smashed it by clapping my hands together. I looked at it. It was a male; it had the feathery proboscis.

In that old movie *The Fly*, Jeff Goldblum was half fly, half man. When I was so sick, that's kind of what I felt like. I felt like I was turning into something that wasn't me. Some scientists wanted to eradicate all the mosquitoes in the world, because they thought only good could come of that and it would prevent diseases like dengue, West Nile virus, and malaria. I wondered if that was true or whether every living thing had a purpose.

"What are you doing in here?" I asked the smashed mosquito.

"Obaachan, Summer is talking to dead mosquitoes again," Jaz said, causing Obaachan to laugh.

Then Obaachan stopped laughing and said, "Summer and Jaz always make me forget pain."

The supermarket was air-conditioned. Basically, it was paradise. Except for two cashiers at the front, it was totally empty as far as I could see. I didn't get to go to a supermarket very often. At home we just went to the local grocer's in town. There had been a big sign outside saying GRAND OPENING. Below that it said IF YOU BUILD IT, THEY WILL COME.

I was kind of surprised by just how big this store was, and how empty. Obaachan handed me some recipes for the rest of the week. I had to get all the ingredients that weren't crossed out.

Mrs. Parker had miscalculated how much cereal everybody would eat. I put five boxes of Cheerios into my cart. Original Cheerios was the bestselling cereal in the country. It had been invented in 1941 and was called Cheerioats until 1945. I knew this because we once had to do a paper on one of the top ten crops raised in Kansas. Oats were much less important to the economy of Kansas than wheat, but I chose to write about oats because I figured I already knew a lot about wheat, and I just felt like learning something new. There were something like twelve different types of Cheerios the last time I counted.

In the dairy section I found buttermilk, fat-free milk, flavored milk, lactose-free milk, low-fat milk, reduced-fat milk, whole milk, almond milk, coconut milk, rice milk, and soy milk. Mrs. Parker wanted 2 percent milk. This really annoyed Obaachan because she was a firm believer in whole milk, especially for growing kids. So I bought an extra carton of regular milk for Jaz and me, even though it wasn't on the list and even though Mrs. Parker had told Obaachan to get exactly what was on the list. I guess we were already going rogue.

Then we bought all the other stuff and checked out while the cashier smiled almost the whole time, even when nobody was talking. Then she smiled harder and said, "Thank you. We hope to see you again!"

The whole way back, Obaachan was growling "Errrr," so I knew she was in a lot of pain. She took seven aspirin, then said, "If I die from aspirin poisoning, Parker fire us. Here. Take this." She pulled over and handed the cell phone to me.

When we got a signal, I helped Obaachan call Mrs. Parker. "We almost back," she told her. "Yes . . . Yes . . . Yes . . . Yes . . . Yes . . . Good-bye." She handed the phone back to me. "Make sure that turned off."

I looked at the phone. "It's turned off."

"If you wrong and she hear me, you grounded. I keeping list of every time you grounded during harvest. Then you be grounded for long time."

"It's off," I said again.

"I just want to say, then. I want to say that woman drive me crazy."

"Well, she's just very detail-oriented," I said.

"I like detail too. I love detail! Detail my most

favorite thing in world! But she drive me crazy."

When we arrived at the Laskey farm, it was already afternoon. The combines were going strong. When we got back to the camper, I called in on the radio. "Mrs. Parker? We're back. Should we make everyone sandwiches?"

"Yes, of course. I've decided to move dinner to eight for this job."

"Okay."

"Personally, I believe in three nice, big meals a day, not in those six smaller meals that are so popular today."

"Yes, ma'am."

"Personally, I believe in the traditional method of just about anything."

Obaachan was watching me glumly. "Yes, ma'am," I told Mrs. Parker.

"I'd like to get on one of those cooking shows. I think my recipes are just as good. I looked into self-publishing a cookbook; I think it would be a bestseller."

"Yes, ma'am."

"Anyway, you'd better get to making the sandwiches."

"Yes, ma'am."

I put the radio down.

Obaachan was pressing her palms against her temples. "She give detail a bad name."

Obaachan made the sandwiches and went to drive them out to the combines. I went into the bedroom and took out my lucky amber, with the mosquito in it. I pressed it against my forehead for luck and then meditated the way Jiichan had taught me. First I did alternating-nostril deep breathing, then I lay down on my back and spread out my limbs. Thunder took that as an invitation and climbed back and forth over me three times before settling down on my shins. Jiichan liked me to pick a person to open my heart to. I picked Jenson. "I accept you for who you are," I said. I hadn't even realized he was still in my mind, but apparently, he was. I tried to picture him. But usually when I closed my eyes, all I saw were chaotic lights and shapes. Mrs. Parker once said she could see pages and pages of writing in her head if she'd just read a book. She could pick out a page number and know exactly what was on that page.

After I did my breathing, I opened my heart to Jaz, as Jiichan sometimes asked me to do. Then I tried to untangle some of what I saw when I closed my eyes. I could never quite meditate because of the chaos in my head. After a while I thought I was awake . . . unless I was asleep. The next thing I knew, Jaz was leaning his face a foot over mine.

"Hey, Summer?" Jaz asked.

"You surprised me!" I yelped.

"Two kids at school said I'm a freak."

"Which two kids?"

"Just two kids."

"You're not a freak," I said.

"Why do you think they said it, then?"

"Because they don't know what they're talking about," I told him firmly.

"Summer, can you just answer honestly?"

I considered that and decided to tell him what my true opinion was at that moment. "I think you're a very intense boy and are really good at concentrating, and Jiichan says people like that are very successful in life."

"Like thinking hard can make me successful?" Jaz asked. Something in his voice indicated that he was already moving on from the idea that he was a freak and was now playing with the possibility that he was a great thinker.

"Yes."

"That's interesting," he said, clearly pondering which particular type of greatness he should aspire to.

I could hear voices in the kitchen and realized Robbie was talking to Obaachan. I really wanted to go out there to see Robbie, but Jaz's earnest expression—with a few scars on his forehead— told me that he needed my full attention right then.

"So why can't I make friends with any kids from school?"

Trying to be helpful, I said, "Sometimes you say the wrong things at the wrong time." I heard Robbie saying, "Okay, thanks, bye," then I heard the door open and close. Rats.

"How can you say the wrong thing at the wrong time?" Jaz asked me. "If you have a thought, why not say it?"

"It's like that time the teacher said you started singing during a test."

"I got an A on that test."

I ignored that and said, "There was that time we went into town and you asked that boy from your class if he wanted to come over and play." I felt the camper shake from the wind. Tonight would be dry and windy. The dust and bits of cut wheat would make the combines look like gigantic tumbleweeds.

"What was wrong with asking him that?"

"You can't just ask someone that."

"Why?"

"Because he's not your friend yet."

"How can he become my friend if he doesn't come over?"

Jaz was making my brain hurt. I heard Obaachan growling and pushed myself up, then pulled my knees in close and rested my chin on them. I didn't know what to say. He was a strange boy.

"You'll make another friend," I said finally. "It just might take time." I stood up. "I have to help Obaachan. You coming?"

"No."

In the kitchen Obaachan was making lasagna. She didn't even turn her head. "You make brownies," she ordered.

"How did you know it was me?"

"I have eyes on back of head."

I took out the mixing bowl. "You always lecture me to tell the truth."

"I never lie."

"But you just said you have eyes on the back of your head."

"Did I know who come in without looking?"

"Yes."

"Then I no lie."

At almost eight, we drove dinner out to the combines. I'd seen Robbie on a dirt bike ahead of us. At the combines, Obaachan and I arranged all the food on the open bed of the pickup, buffet style. We'd set out a bunch of folding canvas chairs for everyone. The drivers all stretched their necks and backs before turning to the food.

"It's lasagna," I said proudly, even though I hadn't made it. "And brownies for dessert."

Mrs. Parker was already looking over the food. "Oh, dear, the broccoli is overcooked." She turned to me and Obaachan. "If there's one thing I hate, it's overcooked vegetables. Wasn't that included in the directions at the start of my menu book?"

117

Obaachan didn't say a thing, so that left it to me to admit, "We didn't get a chance to read the whole preface. The broccoli is still kind of crunchy."

"Oh, honey, you must read the preface. It's my whole theory of cooking. I just wrote it this year. It needs to be a tad crunchier."

"I'm sorry. I'll read it, I promise." I felt totally deflated. She leaned over and lightly sniffed the lasagna but didn't comment. She only glanced at the brownies.

Everybody grabbed the reusable plastic plates and utensils and sat down. I stood watching. Mick stuck a big forkful of lasagna in his mouth, then made an unpleasant face. When he had swallowed, he said, "A bit cheesy, isn't it?" Right then and there, I decided I hated Mick.

Mrs. Parker looked offended. "It's my own personal recipe." Then she took a bite, smacked her mouth together a few times, and shook her head. "Oh, no, no, no. This is all wrong. Too much Parmesan and no basil at all."

Since Obaachan obviously wasn't going to participate in this conversation, I said, "There actually wasn't any fresh basil at the store."

Finally, Obaachan said, "Not enough Parmesan in your recipe. Lasagna need—what you call it?—tang. I put more in."

Mrs. Parker looked at Obaachan as if she couldn't believe her ears. There was a deadly silence.

Then Mr. Parker said, "Oh, come on, honey, it's actually good. I like the tang."

She looked at him as if she was going to take a butcher knife and plunge it into his heart.

"Tang. No tang. All I know is this is good food and I'm hungry," he said. "Sit down and eat, sweetheart. Mick, cheese is good for you."

Mrs. Parker turned to Obaachan. "This must be the last time, and I do mean the last, that you deviate from a recipe."

Obaachan said, "What 'deviate'?"

"It means change," Mrs. Parker answered. "You must follow my recipes exactly. I just want you to know that before I married my husband, I went to cooking school and worked as a chef for seven years."

Obaachan nodded her head and said, "You great cook. I know that. But your school no teach you about tang."

I was stunned that Obaachan would talk back to Mrs. Parker.

"In future I follow all your recipe exactly," Obaachan continued. "But I have very strong feeling about tang. But you pay me, I leave the tang out. I give you my promise."

I'd never even heard Obaachan use the word "tang" before.

Obaachan and I sat down and began eating with the others. It really wasn't half bad. Yes, it had more tang than the usual lasagna, but it still tasted good. Everybody scarfed down their food. All the guys even went for seconds. Then it was brownie time. Nobody commented as they ate their brownies, so I guess that was good. Personally, I thought they were excellent brownies.

Then Robbie suddenly said, "Good brownies."

"I made them," I said. And I had to admit, they were *excellent*.

I wanted to make him brownies every day for the rest of the harvest.

# CHAPTER EIGHT

The next morning I woke up first to cook. It was Sunday, so that made it a full-breakfast day, with all twelve of us looking forward to our weekly treat. I was still in a happy mood because Robbie had liked my brownies. In fact, I started to think that perhaps they were the best brownies I had ever tasted. And to tell the truth, I mistakenly put in a little more sugar than the recipe called for.

Jiichan walked into the kitchen and stared at the pan I planned to use to scramble thirty eggs. It was made of Teflon. We didn't have anything made of Teflon at home because Jiichan refused to eat anything cooked on weird pots and pans that were coated with who knew what kind of chemicals. Jiichan stumbled backward with a hand on his heart. I knew it was because of the Teflon. I waited for him to recover. "Don't worry," I said. I took out a smaller stainless-steel pan to cook his three sunny-side-up eggs in, using the special oil we'd brought for him—a mix of butter from grass-fed cows, organic coconut oil, and organic extra-virgin olive oil. Jiichan ate as much junk food as anyone, but he balanced it with this magical oil.

Unfortunately, dishwashing was one of my chores both at home and on harvest, so I had scraped quite a few pans in my life and pretty much thought that whoever had invented Teflon had done the world a big favor. I wondered if the inventor of Teflon was someone like Jaz, some brainy dude locked up in a lab twelve hours a day while he chewed gum and blew bubbles exactly the same size, over and over.

"I got very bad feel about Teflon," Jiichan said. "Teflon invented by someone who care more about easy than about good."

I cooked everyone else's eggs at the same time

and toasted and buttered a loaf of wheat bread. I fried thirty sausages and started the coffee and the hot water for tea. I radioed the Parkers. "Breakfast is ready," I said. Then I felt kind of shy about going over to the drivers' quarters. Finally, I crept forward and peered into their room. "Breakfast," I said, but not loudly enough to wake anyone. I took a big breath. "Breakfast!" I said, even more loudly than I'd meant to.

"Girl, we're not deaf," Mick said. The guys started getting out of bed, some of them in their underwear. For half a second I stared, but then I hurried from the room. There was hair all over their chests! A lot!

Obaachan was setting the kitchen table. Breakfast was always indoors, I didn't know why. I guess that was just the way Mrs. Parker liked it. No harvesting operation I had ever heard of cooked a hot breakfast for the workers, even on Sundays. But like I said, the Parkers had started out as drivers themselves, so they really liked to take good care of their team.

Rory, Sean, and Mick came into the kitchen at the same time. I sat down with my plate and slid to the very end of one of the benches. I didn't know whether I wanted Robbie to sit next to me or not. It was kind of stressful sitting next to him. On the other hand, it was also fun and exciting. Mick took some eggs and five sausages and slid in next to me. He hadn't bothered brushing his hair, and tufts of it stood up on his head.

"Summer. What's the craic?" he said.

But I couldn't stop staring at his plate. *Who eats five sausages?* I thought. Now there were only twenty-five left for everyone else. But I could make that work by not eating any until after everyone else had eaten theirs.

"Summer?" Mick asked.

"The usual," I replied. "Got up at six."

"Summer, is there milk in it?" Rory asked.

"Yes, in the fridge." I forgot what exactly "in it" meant to Irish people, but it didn't exactly mean "in it" like we thought.

"Jaykers! Ya want milk? The amount of milk ya drink, ya're going to turn into a cow," Mick exclaimed.

"What's that? I like milk, all right? My ma always gave me a lot."

"Ah, still a mama's boy, are ya, then?" Mick teased.

"I like milk, sure. It doesn't make me a mama's boy," Rory retorted, slipping in next to Mick.

"Well, these long days'll make a man out of ya."

"If it doesn't break him," Sean said, thumping his plate on the table. Sean had taken four sausages. Well, the sausage situation wasn't my fault. I had made exactly as many sausages as Mrs. Parker had said to in her binder.

Obaachan poured a glass of milk for Rory and passed it down to him.

I felt more comfortable with them than with the two American drivers. I wasn't sure why, but maybe it was because I felt closer in the pecking order to the Irish guys. The Americans were older, so I had to show them more respect.

Mrs. Parker swept into the camper, her chin rising a bit as she sniffed the air, a lot like Thunder would do.

I looked over at Jiichan and saw him closing his eyes the way he often did when eating. It was like he was savoring his magic oil.

I didn't know what to say, so I kept it basic.

"So what's it like where you guys live?" I asked the Irishmen.

"Oh, it's lovely, beautiful countryside," Mick replied, his voice suddenly catching fire. He was the most talkative of the three.

"Tell her about yer crop circles, then," Rory said, elbowing him with a laugh.

"Ya can make fun about it, but it's an honest day's work," Mick shot back, returning the elbow.

"Last year, and the year before that, he took people on tours of crop circles all over Ireland," Rory explained, setting down his fork. "Mostly Americans, and he charges them a thousand euro a tour. He probably makes the circles by himself!"

Mick chewed on a sausage, unperturbed. He swallowed and turned toward me. "It's a mystery, and they want to see a mystery. I join together a mystery and someone who wants to see a mystery. That's all it is." He spoke wearily, as if he had said this many times before. It struck me that he was basically a salesman, selling a mystery to Americans. He then speared another sausage and put the whole thing in his mouth at once.

Rory laughed loudly. "He can talk for an hour

about nothing but crop circles. But don't get him started, because he might bore ya to death."

"I don't even know what a crop circle is," I said.

Rory groaned. "Now ya're going to get him started." Rory was a skinny guy with curly red hair—on his head *and* his chest!

Robbie entered the kitchen next, asking, "Is there coffee?" Obaachan said I couldn't drink coffee because it would stunt my growth. I wondered if she was taking note of how tall Robbie was. Although, I have to say that once, Obaachan had let me taste some, and it was so awful I had no plans to ever drink any again. I had been looking forward to drinking coffee my whole life, but after that I had to cross it off my list of things I wanted to do one day. Actually, I didn't really have a list. It was more like things I made mental notes of. Right then I made a mental note to start keeping a list of things I wanted to do one day. Honestly, I would be happy if I could just visit the Badlands once a month or so. I think that would help me settle my personality.

Mick leaned forward and said, "Robbie, can

ya get me a couple of sausages?" That meant he was eating seven sausages so far. Seven! Then he turned back to me. "A crop circle is a huge, geometric pattern that appears in a field, usually a wheat field. They're mostly in England, but we get them in Ireland, too," he said.

"So why do people want to see them?" I asked. I saw Mrs. Parker leaning over the sausages and counting.

"Because no one knows how they got there. Every one is different, and some are as big as two or three hundred meters. Even the complicated ones are perfectly symmetrical," he said, starting to get excited. "We don't know if it's the earth trying to communicate with us or what."

"Some people are gobshites," Rory said. "Gobshites" were gullible people. I had picked that up during the last harvest we'd worked. "But ya know, I think Mick is becoming a gobshite too. He actually believes everything he tells his customers."

Jiichan looked up from his plate. "What 'gobshite'?"

"It's someone gullible," I told him.

Jiichan looked surprised. "Nothing wrong with gullible. How you be happy if not gullible?"

Everyone looked at him silently for a moment, but he didn't explain.

"Some circles are not a mystery. They're made by humans as hoaxes. But others are mysterious, to be sure," Mick went on defensively. "Personally, I believe the earth is talking to us, but we don't know what it's saying."

"Tell her about that one couple, Micky," Rory said.

Mick set his fork on the table. "One American couple gave me a four-hundred-euro tip at the end of the tour. Can ya believe it? They said they were transformed, they did."

"Ya're such an eejit," Rory said. He hit the top of Mick's head with his palm.

"What's an eejit?" I asked.

"Ya know, an eejit. Someone who's lacking in the brain department."

"Oh, an idiot."

"That would be himself."

Mr. Parker walked in. "How'd you sleep, boys?" he asked. "It was so windy, our camper was shaking. Hard to get a good night's rest."

"Nobody can sleep, anyway, because Rory snores so loud," Sean said, almost ruthlessly. "He's useless, he is."

"He's an excellent worker," Mr. Parker said.

"Ah, teacher's pet," Sean said to Rory.

Mr. McCoy rambled in, looking seriously like he needed more sleep. I felt bad for him. He even swayed a bit as if he were going to fall over. He took three sausages, and then Mr. Dark came in and took three more. Then Mick asked for more. Unbelievable.

Jiichan started chuckling. Everyone fell silent, again waiting for him to explain. But he didn't say anything. Then he began laughing quite hard. Everybody was looking at him. "Got a good joke, then, Toshiro?" Mick said.

Jiichan looked at Mick in surprise. "Joke?"

"It's just that ya were laughing so much," Mick replied.

Jiichan said, "Oh, I laugh because one day two year ago, I drive all the way to grocery store before I remember I no need grocery. I supposed to go to dentist."

"That no funny," Obaachan said. "We have to pay dentist for missed appointment."

There was another brief silence at the table.

Mr. Parker reached for four sausages. Finally, Mrs. Parker couldn't stand it anymore. "How many sausages were cooked?" she blurted out.

"We made thirty, like you instructed," I answered.

Robbie sat down and drank his coffee just like a grown-up.

Obviously slightly annoyed with me, Mrs. Parker said, "Well, Robbie loves meat. It's his favorite part of breakfast. For this one thing, I give you permission to alter the number of sausages specified."

"Yes, boys need meat. Very important," Obaachan said. "It very bad tragedy if he no have meat for breakfast." She shook her head. "Tragedy, tragedy."

I knew Obaachan was being serious, because boys needing meat was one of her most important rules in life. But Mrs. Parker couldn't seem to tell if Obaachan was agreeing with her or mocking her.

Mr. Parker pushed away his plate and said, "We're in a tight situation here. One of our customers up in Oklahoma called this morning before dawn to say their wheat is ready to cut. And they're expecting rain. We'll need to work late tonight—probably until two again. If we don't get up there soon enough, I'll have to find other cutters to take our place, and I don't want to lose that job." He stood up and glanced around. Even though Jiichan hadn't finished eating, he got up and stretched his back and neck to ready himself for work. Jiichan ate very slowly, so I was worried he hadn't gotten enough to eat.

Mr. Parker didn't say another word, but all the other workers got up too and readied themselves to leave, taking along the sandwiches I had already prepared for them for lunch.

Everyone left at once, except for Robbie. Obaachan got on all fours, resting the top of her head on the linoleum. This was something new. Robbie watched her with interest. I started stacking the dirty breakfast plates.

"Obaachan, are you okay?" I asked.

"No, I think I dying. This is it. Don't forget

make more meat next Sunday. If I die, I won't be here to remind you."

Robbie was studying my grandmother. "Shouldn't she go to a doctor?" he asked.

"She's gone to seventeen different doctors, six chiropractors, and three acupuncturists, and nobody knows exactly what's causing the pain."

I turned to place the plates in the sink.

"Don't you ever stop working?" Robbie asked.

I spun around and was startled by how close he was. He was about a foot away from me, right inside my personal space. "Cooking is supposed to be my grandmother's job, but she's got her horrible back pains. She fell on her back when she was a little girl, but she wouldn't tell me how. Jiichan said, however, that she fell climbing out of a window. He didn't enlighten me as to why she was climbing out this window, but clearly she had been a troublemaker." I could feel my face in flames.

He looked at me in a perfectly normal fashion, as if girls always blushed fiercely when they talked to him. I swallowed some saliva. Next he took out a quarter from his pocket, flipped it into the air, and caught it before slapping it on the table. He looked at the coin. "Heads. I guess I'm doing schoolwork." He lingered a moment. "Are you going to cook Japanese for us one day?"

"We're doing *shabu-shabu* one day. Your mom said we could."

"What's *shabu-shabu*?"

"It's thick noodles with thinly sliced beef and vegetables. I mean, the vegetables aren't thinly sliced. You cook it in a pot in front of you, and after you're done eating, you drink the broth, and, oh, I forgot to mention there are two sauces you dip everything in, and it's just so good. We brought the sauces with us from home, and we're going to cook it all on the stove before serving it. We even brought our special meat slicer. The reason we own a slicer is that my mother works cooking in a hunting lodge in the off-season, and a lot of the customers there like *shabu-shabu*, so we need the meat slicer for that. It's a really good one. We paid, like, a million dollars for it, because we eat *shabu-shabu* once a week." I couldn't get myself to shut up. I was babbling like an eejit! I pressed down on my lips to keep myself from talking more.

"I had some cooked sashimi once in Oklahoma. It was pretty good."

"Uh-huh," I said. Cooked sashimi didn't make sense, because sashimi meant "raw fish." It was like saying cooked raw carrots. But I didn't want to insult him. "I mean, it's kind of unusual, but unusual things are really cool because of their unusualness, even if they're, you know, unusual." I was sounding dimmer by the moment.

"Do you want me to show you something amazing at the barn?"

I glanced at Obaachan, the top of her head still resting on the floor. "Sure, yes." I went rushing out the door before Obaachan had a chance to stop me. Thunder, as always, followed me.

Was this a date? That thought made me take off my apron and stuff as much of it as I could into my back pocket. We strolled toward the barn, which was made of some kind of reddish wood. The roof was painted brick red. When we went inside, we stopped in front of a blond bull in a standing stock in the middle of the barn. "They're going to enter him in the state fair," Robbie said. "He's one of those bulls they wash and blow-dry and all that to get them ready. They put a little rose water on him too, but just a small bit. They want him to smell good, but not girly. They even trim some of his hairs."

I wondered how Robbie knew so much about this bull. "My grandfather worked as a cattle fitter for a while. He's a nice-looking bull," I said. "But he's not standing right."

"They hired another fitter to help with that," Robbie said. I nodded. "But that's not what I wanted to show you," he continued.

We passed a few stalls until he stopped at an especially big one. And there stood the tallest horse I'd ever seen. Maybe it was an illusion, but he looked like he could be twenty hands. I knew he couldn't possibly be that tall, because the tallest horse in history was about twenty-one hands. I had read that in my brother's list of the biggest animals in history. He'd made the list when he was eight years old.

"Cool, huh?" Robbie said. He rested his face on a metal bar. He seemed in awe.

"I saw a huge shire horse at a county fair once, but this one is definitely bigger," I said. This horse was black with white feet and a skimpy black mane. He eyed us calmly.

"The height's in his legs," Robbie said. "They're so long, he looks kind of gawky. Usually shires are stockier."

We stood awhile. I felt like time had stopped in here, like we were kind of floating in time. Robbie stepped back from the stall and touched my upper arm, making it tingle. "I better get to studying," he said. "I have a whole algebra workbook I have to finish over the summer. I love algebra. I think about it all the time."

Ugh. Algebra. I mean, all I thought about was my family, Thunder, my friends, and mosquitoes that killed maybe a million people a year—a million people!—but struck about three hundred million. Did you ever wonder how many diseases are carried by mosquitoes? I never did, until I got sick, and now I sure as heck know. Besides malaria, dengue, and encephalitis, mosquitoes can spread a couple of disgusting worms: helminth parasitic worms and dog heartworm, like my previous dog, Shika, had had. But not every mosquito carries diseases. Many of them are kind of innocent, for mosquitoes.

Anyway. We stepped back out into the sunshine, a warm breeze blowing into my face. Robbie was closing the barn door when I realized that Thunder wasn't with us. "Wait, where's my dog? We must have left him inside." Robbie pulled open the door. I didn't see Thunder, and there was nowhere to hide, just the long row of stalls, with the standing stock in the center. Still, I called out,

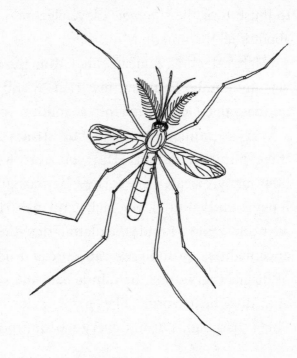

"Thunder! Thunder, come!" I went back outside. "Thunder! C'mere, boy!"

Robbie was scanning the yard. "I don't see him anywhere."

"Weird. He's very good about coming when I call. I trained him really well." But as I said that, a feeling of dread hit me out of the blue. It was immediately followed by a ruckus that sounded like a bunch of chickens going crazy. I ran like mad toward the sound, but I already knew what I'd find.

On the other side of the barn, chickens were squawking all over the place. And there was Thunder, holding a speckled hen in his mouth, shaking it wildly. He looked ecstatic.

"No!" I shouted. "Down!" He pranced away. "No. Bad boy! Stay!" I stomped toward him and grabbed both sides of the chicken hanging out of his mouth. "No!" I yanked the chicken out and threw it down. Then I turned to assess the damage. It looked like there were three dead birds. "Bad dog! Bad, bad dog!" Thunder cowered and whined.

"Let's get out of here," Robbie said urgently.

He ran off, and I followed, holding Thunder firmly by the collar. This wasn't the first time that he'd killed chickens—it had happened once at a neighbor's farm back home. The farmer had said that the best way to cure a dog of killing chickens was to tie a dead chicken around its neck for a week and let the chicken rot. My parents had refused to do that, and fortunately, Thunder had not ventured into the neighbor's farm again.

But this was worse—much, much worse—because for a cook or a combine driver, the farmer was like the king. When we reached the campers, we came to a halt, looking around furtively.

Robbie laid a hand on my shoulder. "I'm sorry. It's my fault," he said. "It was all my idea."

"No, Thunder's my responsibility. I should have kept my eye on him. I can't believe I didn't." I thought of all the times my mother had said to me, "Summer, what were you thinking?" This time I knew exactly what I had been thinking—how cute Robbie was.

"Okay, listen," Robbie said, dropping his voice. "I didn't see anyone else around. Unless someone saw us, it should be okay. Just don't tell anyone."

"We have to tell someone! Someone has to pay for the dead chickens."

*"Don't—tell—anyone,"* he warned. "I don't want my parents getting in trouble." He glared at me, then turned and walked away.

"See ya," I called out, but he didn't answer.

# CHAPTER NINE

I stepped inside our camper dragging Thunder with me while Robbie went wherever he went, probably to his camper to study and get ready for college. Obaachan was standing up, already boiling oxtails for stew. The remnants of breakfast were gone. She glanced at me and said, "You with Robbie. He no good for boyfriend. Anyone who think you can eat cooked sashimi have problem in head. He need psychiatrist." She wanted to talk about sashimi now? Now when my entire life might have just been ruined? It was ruined because I knew I had to tell Obaachan or Jiichan about the chickens, and then Robbie would hate me. But I didn't see why the Laskeys would be mad at Robbie's parents. It wasn't their fault at all.

I just stood there and stared at her. I knew I had to confess to what Thunder had done.

Jaz was working on his LEGO apartment building at the kitchen table, adding "Cooked sashimi?" He laughed lightheartedly. "Sometimes I'm glad you're my sister. Your life is nutty." He laughed more. Then he seemed to be thinking. "But why would anyone want to be your boyfriend?" he asked. He looked at me innocently. "Seriously."

"Why is every day Pick on Summer Day?" I asked.

"No. No. I'm not trying to insult you," Jaz said. "I was just curious."

Unfortunately, I couldn't think of a single reason why a boy would want to be my boyfriend. Some girls in my class already had boyfriends. They wore makeup and had cell phones and polished their nails. I tried to polish my nails once, and it smelled so horrible, I knew I could never do that again. Then I thought of one reason I'd make a good girlfriend. "I'm a good cook," I said triumphantly.

"Men don't care about good cook until ready to

get married," Obaachan said. "You think fourteen-year-old boy want you to roast him chicken?"

I pressed my lips together and looked at my flip-flops.

Obaachan set down her stirring spoon. "What you thinking about?" she asked.

"Nothing."

"I know you thinking," she said. "Remember, I can see inside your head."

"Well, I'm always thinking. I wasn't thinking about anything special. If you could really see inside my head, you'd know I wasn't thinking about anything special."

"I only see shapes and writing in your head, but I no can read the writing because it too messy. You tell me what writing say. I see shape of something bad."

I wondered if it was shaped like a dead chicken. I'd actually rather tell Jiichan than Obaachan, but Jiichan wouldn't be finished working until two in the morning. I looked down at my flip-flops again. What if something terrible happened, like Obaachan made me get rid of Thunder?

"Something happened," I said.

"Something happen every day."

"It's really all my fault. It isn't Thunder's fault, and it isn't Robbie's fault. It's all mine, one hundred percent," I said passionately.

"Tell me what it is," Obaachan said. "But I warn you, you tell me something that give me heart attack, my death on your conscience forever."

I looked directly at Obaachan. "Well, I went with Robbie to look at a gigantic horse in the Laskeys' stable. He was really huge. And I forgot all about Thunder, and he got to where the free-range chickens are . . . and . . . killed three of them." I felt my eyes filling with tears.

Obaachan snapped, "Tears don't change my heart." Then she got down on all fours again, the top of her head against the floor. "*Hara* tell me all I need to know about that boy," she said.

*Hara* means "stomach" or "gut." Although Japanese do think with their hearts or heads like anyone, for them, thinking with your gut was a whole different level of thinking. My grandfather was always telling me, "Think with your *hara*!"

"Obaachan, it wasn't his fault," I exclaimed. It

wasn't. "I'm the one who should have been watching Thunder."

Thunder hung his head.

"Nothing no happen without Robbie."

"That doesn't make it his fault." I watched her for a moment. I wondered if this getting on all fours meant her back was getting even worse. "Why are you doing that?"

"Because my body tell me to. I no say it his fault. It your fault." She pushed herself up with a grunt. "You tell the Parkers at dinner. Now you and Jaz do homework. When buzzer go, turn off oven and take out pie. Keep eye on stew. Turn off in four hour exactly to get all the taste into water. Make sure you exact, or Mrs. Parker fire us."

She pushed herself up and walked toward our bedroom, stopping to turn around and look directly at me. "You go study."

"Okay."

"I know what you thinking. You thinking about that boy. You thinking you find that boy. You thinking you do anything except study."

"Obaachan, I honestly wasn't thinking anything. I didn't have time."

"That what you were going to think, even if you didn't think yet."

I rolled my head around. "Obaachan, it's really not fair to get mad at me for something I didn't even think yet."

"I know your brain. You study, or I put more grounding on list I keeping. For killing chicken, you get six-week grounding."

I turned to Jaz. "*You* better study too."

"What did I do?"

I looked to the shelf where we kept Mrs. Parker's binders. That's where we also kept our schoolbooks. I picked out my math book and set it in front of me on the table. I moved my hands closer to it. I couldn't open it, though. I willed my hands to open it. But I still couldn't do it. Then I returned it to the shelf and took down my history book. I'll bet all sorts of things happened in history that were more interesting than the stuff in this book. In fact, I was sure of it, because Jiichan was reading my history book once and said, "This not history. This public relation document."

Jaz took down his math workbook and was immediately so engrossed, he probably wouldn't even have noticed if there was a tornado—he'd just keep working while he was swirling around in the air.

I decided not to read my history book, so I took down my journal. I was supposed to write about my experiences on harvest for my new teacher, and I would read some of them to the class so they could learn about this lifestyle. But they all knew about it already. We lived in farm country. So what could I say? I had a crush on a boy and Thunder killed some chickens? I cooked sausages? I sat down and tapped my pen on the journal. Then I wrote.

> When you are on harvest, you don't care much about what is going on in the world. What is Congress doing? What is the president doing? I have no idea. All you care about is cutting that wheat as quickly and ~~effish~~ efficiently as you can. You are in another world. I like being in this world because the motto of U.S. Custom Harvesters, Inc., is "We harvest the crops that feed the

148

world." If not for us, many people wouldn't have bread.

That was lame. I drew a line through it and turned the page to start again.

The thing about being a kid is that you don't get to make any decisions on harvest. You just work all the time. I help cook for the crew because my grandmother, who is supposed to be cooking, isn't well.

I drew a line through that too. Then I closed my journal and put it back on the shelf.

I took down paper and *A Separate Peace* to write my book report. The teacher said to sum up your feelings about the book in the first paragraph. Then tell what happened and also mention what you do or don't have in common with the main character. Also, somewhere in there you're supposed to state how the main character changes in the story.

My sixth-grade teacher hated contractions. We were supposed to write, for instance, "do not" rather than "don't." One thing I didn't understand was punctuation. My teacher always said to put your punctuation where it "feels" right. But then when I did that, she always marked up my paper because she said the punctuation was all wrong. Fortunately, the main thing was to mix up descriptions of the book with your own feelings, not to have perfect punctuation. You had to write at least three drafts and hand in all three.

For draft number one, here's what I wrote:

I thought *A Separate Peace* was a
strange and kind of amazing book.
It was very ~~quite~~ quiet, and then
suddenly, it was not quiet at all. So
then the parts that are not quiet make
all the quiet parts seem like they
are not quiet after all. Once I read
the whole book, my mind flashed
back through the whole book again.
It is a book about two boys, Finny
and Gene, and they are best friends.
They are in high school. They go to
a boarding school. It is during World

War II. I am only twelve years old,
so I ~~don't~~ do not know much about
World War II.


This book starts at the end not the
beginning. Most of the book takes
place fifteen years earlier than it is in
the first and last chapters. The main
character, is Gene. Gene used to have
fear when he went to school, but, he
then gets rid of his fear. This was very
interesting to me, because I am scared
of a lot of things. Sometimes, I just
want to stay locked up in my room
at night, because I think a mosquito
might bite me. And, I am afraid, to
ride my bicycle in the night, even
though I have my dog, Thunder, with
me and even if I am covered in DEET.
Even if a mosquito does not bite me,
who knows a car might hit me.
For Gene, there was a very important
insident that happened fifteen years
earlier. If anyone reads this report and

has not read the book yet, consider this, a \*spoiler alert\*. Finny climbs up a tree and when he is on a branch, Gene shakes the branch and Finny falls.

Finny used to be, a great athelete, but now his leg is broken so bad from the fall that he cannot be an athelete anymore. Later in the book Finny falls down a set of stairs. Then, he dies during ~~sugary~~ surgery on his leg. The problem is, I do not really understand if Gene could have possibly shook the branch on purpose. I mean, who would do that to their best friend? Gene was jealous of how good an athelete Finny is, so I guess Gene, shakes the branch on purpose to hurt Finny??

Before Finny dies, then Gene starts to dress like Finny. Finny trains

Gene to be an athelete like Finny
used to be. Gene becomes like Finny
because Finny cannot be himself
anymore. This is insane behavior in
my opinion. Their relationship is so
intense that it is insane.

Finny dies. Then Gene can start to act
like himself again.

I stopped writing. We were supposed to write
the theme or the lesson of the book at the end of
the report. I didn't understand what the theme or
lesson of this book could be. I thought about it,
and then I started writing again.

People are very complicated, and
I do not think even a really smart
~~psichyatrist psyciatrist~~ psychiatrist
can truly figure out what is in your
brain and what is in your heart or
stomach. You might not even realize
it, but maybe you would shake
a branch your best friend is on,

although I personally do not think I would ever do that. ~~Your~~ My brain and heart might be mixed up and tangled, and inside of ~~you~~ me there are both good and bad things. The lesson of *A Separate Peace* is that it ~~takes~~ might take fifteen years to untangle all those things inside of me.

I must say I thought that was a pretty brilliant book report. Plus, the book really gave me insight into life. It made me realize that since I was twelve, I could be almost twenty-seven by the time I was untangled. That seemed like an awfully long time in the future, but maybe there was a way to shorten the time. I knew you would have to work hard at it, because if it was easy to untangle yourself, everybody would be untangled, which simply isn't true.

Anyway, it was time to start adding carrots and potatoes to the stew. Jiichan had told me that while I was cooking, I should put love into what I was doing, and then the food would be healthier. I couldn't find my apron, so I put on Obaachan's. I picked up a knife to slice the potatoes. How did I put love into that? I thought, *I love everyone, I love everyone, I love everyone.* I kept thinking that while I sliced. I held my open palms over the potatoes and thought, *Love, love, love.* I really concentrated. But as hard as I concentrated, I just couldn't feel love for these potatoes.

"What are you doing?" Jaz asked.

"Putting love into the potatoes," I answered.

"Putting love into the potatoes," he repeated.

"Jiichan said to put love into the food as I cook."

Jaz laughed a delighted laugh. I don't know why, but I laughed too.

# CHAPTER TEN

For dinner we drove out to the combines and ate on the canvas chairs, the stew in a big pot on the pickup's lowered gate. I decided to wait until the last minute to tell the Parkers about the dead chickens. If I told them sooner, it might ruin their digestion. On the other hand, I thought about how my grandfather had once told me that when I did something bad, I should try to hurry through it. Like, instead of sitting around worrying about it, just get the confession and punishment over with as quickly as I could. "Make time go faster," he had said.

I kept my eyes on Mrs. Parker as she took her

first sip. She didn't change expressions. She took another sip and said, "Not bad," and my heart leapt. I wondered if she could feel any love in the potatoes. Since the stew had turned out okay, maybe she wouldn't be so upset when I told her about the chickens.

I swear I was just about to confess, but then right toward the end of dinner, Mr. Laskey came by with a pretty girl about my age and said, "Keep your eyes open for coyotes. One of them killed three of my prize chickens in broad daylight. Never saw that before." He shook his head angrily. "And I've got the best free-range chickens in the county. People have paid a hundred dollars for one of my chickens."

Holy moly. Since I had saved $461 in my whole life, that meant my money was only worth four and a half of his chickens.

"Dad," the pretty girl said, "can I have some of their pie?"

But he wasn't looking at her. He was looking at me. Mr. Laskey's eyes had fallen on mine while he said "never saw that before," and I could hardly breathe. It was as if he were talking directly to me, like somehow he knew who was responsible. It was time to confess. But I couldn't get my mouth open. I shot a look at Obaachan to confess for me, but she just sat spooning her stew as if none of this had anything to do with her. Robbie and I met eyes.

Mr. Laskey's daughter, who was standing right next to where I was sitting, was wearing her hair in two braids, just like mine. She had eyelashes so long, they seemed almost unreal. "Hi, I'm Summer," I told her.

"Hi," she said coldly, and I knew right then she didn't want to be friends. I had on an apron, which I guess told her everything she needed to know about me. A part of me wanted to be friends with her, and a part of me wanted to bop her on the head.

"How many days do you think are left?" Mr. Laskey asked Mr. Parker.

There was an awkward silence. Then Mr. Parker said, "Don't worry, we'll get all your wheat cut before the rain. But, uh, up in Oklahoma we have a customer who's expecting rain soon. So we're going to have to split up the team. We'll keep two combines here and send two up to Oklahoma."

Mr. Laskey frowned. "I hired your whole team to cut this wheat, not half your team."

"We'll get it done before it rains here. I guarantee you that," Mr. Parker said. "I've crunched all the numbers. We're working sixteen hours today, and the way it's going, by the end of Tuesday we should have more than four thousand acres cut."

"But rain is expected here," Mr. Laskey said.

"Right, and we'll have already finished your farm. If we don't get your grain in on time, I will personally pay for any wheat that gets wasted," Mr. Parker replied.

Mr. Laskey didn't answer, just drove off with his daughter.

Mr. Parker said impatiently, "All right, we've had enough to eat. Back to work." So even though everybody still had food in their bowls, they all got back into their various machines.

We loaded up the bowls and canvas chairs. Obaachan didn't say a word to me. But later when we had finished cleaning the dishes, and the bowls were stacked in the rack, she said, "I never been so ashamed of you." Then she went to lie down facing south, while the rest of us would sleep north. Maybe I should have started sleeping south as well.

Then I plopped down on the front steps of the camper with Thunder at my feet. I was filled with shame that I hadn't confessed, but now it just seemed impossible that I could. I pushed my hands against my head, hard. It was the sort of thing Jaz might do. I felt like my whole world was filled with nothing but responsibilities and consequences. I didn't even know if I wanted to grow up. I would have even more responsibilities then, even more consequences.

I mean, I knew there were consequences, I knew I had to talk to the Parkers, but I just didn't understand why my life was right here, in this particular place, and why I was the most unamazing person in the world. Why was I the girl wearing an apron?

I thought about going to talk to Mr. Laskey, but it might be that the Parkers would want to explain it themselves. I also thought very seriously about doing nothing at all. Mr. Laskey already thought a coyote was to blame. The only people who knew otherwise were me, Robbie, and Obaachan. Why had I told her? I knocked my hand against my skull and said, "Eejit!"

And what kind of crazy person pays a hundred dollars for a single chicken? I looked up at the stars. Jaz thought that out there in other galaxies, there were other inhabited planets, and that each inhabited planet had its own Bible, and that somewhere in some library in outer space there was something like a galactic *Encyclopaedia Britannica*. I looked back down. I thought of my savings—and of how, after I paid for the chickens, I would have only $161 to show for all the work I'd done in my whole life. A moth landed on me, and I smashed it hard on my arm.

Instantly remorseful, I said, "Sorry, mothie."

I wiped the moth gunk off my arm. Mr. Laskey could afford to lose three hundred dollars more than we could afford it. Dang!

"Come," I said to Thunder, and he followed me into our camper, to our end of it.

Obaachan, who was reading a Japanese magazine, said, "What you want?"

"Obaachan, I can't tell anyone now. Mr. Laskey's already so upset."

"Sometime it very inconvenient to tell truth. But girl I be proud of tell the truth, anyway."

"You are the guilt trip queen!" I shouted at her.

"Grounded for week for yelling at me." She spoke without moving her eyes from the magazine. I made a mental note that I should start keeping track of how much she said she was grounding me. It was adding up.

I pulled my purse from my luggage and took out three hundred dollars. It was a pretty, yellow straw purse with a wooden fish attached to the zipper. I had gotten it for Christmas. I had twenty-one one-dollar bills and the rest in twenties. "Stay," I said to Thunder. "I'm about to do something that's probably really stupid."

I strode across the field toward the farm-house. It was just like a house I would love to live in one day—two stories, a big covered porch, and wicker chairs. They looked so pretty that I went to sit on one for a moment. It would be so nice to sit out here at night and look at the stars.

I thought I heard a noise and jumped up and looked around guiltily. But I didn't see anyone. I knocked on the door.

Mrs. Laskey answered. "Yes?"

I hesitated—Mrs. Laskey didn't look like I would have imagined. Her hair was completely unstyled, not even combed. It was just kind of smooshed on top of her head. And she wore bright red lipstick. Who wore bright red lipstick on a farm? She was exactly my height, five foot one. She looked a little crazy, actually, but in kind of a cute way, like someday she might become Obaachan or Jiichan. That kind of cute . . . although I guess Obaachan wasn't so cute.

"May I speak to Mr. Laskey? I'm with the Parkers."

"Is it something I can help you with?" She gazed at me sincerely, like she really would like to help me.

"It's about the coyotes."

"Oh, all right, then. I'll get him. He's in a war with the coyotes." She invited me inside, then she turned to pick up something from a small table in the foyer. "Would this be yours? It kind of looks like the one you're wearing." She held up a crumpled apron.

I looked at the apron. "Yes, that would be mine." My face burned. I hadn't even realized I'd dropped it. She handed it to me, and I stuffed it into my back pocket.

She studied me for a moment. Then she said, "Don't worry, I won't tell him," and my heart went out to her.

On the table in the foyer there was a lamp that was darkish silver glass interspersed with lighter silver glass in the shape of flowers. I had never seen such a beautiful lamp. I didn't even know anyone made beautiful lamps. I thought lamps were just lamps. It took all my self-control not to lean over and touch it.

Mr. Laskey walked into the foyer. "So you saw the coyotes?" He looked at me as if we were both involved in some kind of conspiracy against those evil coyotes.

"No, sir."

He waited. I stared at him. I had the sudden thought that this was maybe the stupidest idea ever, like, in history. But it was too late now. He started to look puzzled as I just stood there.

"Well, what is it, then, young lady?"

"There are no coyotes," I said sadly. "I mean, there are coyotes, but not here. I mean, not that I know of. My dog killed your chickens, sir." I thrust a wad of bills out to him. "And here's three hundred dollars to pay for them." As I was handing him the money, my intuition told me that he had exaggerated how much his chickens were worth. Only a madman would pay one hundred dollars for a chicken.

I was hoping he wouldn't take the money, but he did. Close up, he seemed so normal, not like someone I should be scared of. His balding head looked soft, and his face looked kind of doughy. And maybe somewhere in that face I saw a hard life. He frowned and counted the money as if I might have cheated him. I waited for him to lecture me. I'd heard many lectures in my life, so I was prepared. "You let your dog run wild in the vicinity of my house?" he asked.

"No, he's always with me. I went to see your giant horse, and I forgot about Thunder—that's my dog—and he found the chickens."

"Where is he now?"

"In the camper. He's confined."

"I want you to keep a good eye on him every second from now on. And I mean every second."

"I will."

"And your parents do what exactly?"

That panicked me a bit—I didn't want Obaachan and Jiichan getting fired. "My grandfather drives a combine and my grandmother is the cook for the crew."

He pulled at his upper lip with a thumb and forefinger. He was quite expert at it and pulled his lip out farther than I would have thought a lip could go. Then he said, "I'll tell you what. I'll take a hundred and leave you the rest." He counted out a hundred dollars and handed the rest to me. "If it happens again, I'll have to ask the Parkers to get rid of the dog."

"Yes, sir. I swear it won't happen again."

But his mind had already moved on. "We tried to get the horse into the record books, but he didn't even make it into the top ten." He flipped out his palms, like, *What are you gonna do?*

"There must be some big horses out there. Anyway, thank you for, uh . . ."

"I appreciate your honesty. Now, run along, young lady."

He was already closing the door as I said, "Good night."

I ran all the way back to our camper. The combines were still churning away, the sound growing louder as they moved nearer, their lights shifting in tandem. I watched for a minute, just kind of smiling to myself. Then I burst into the camper and skipped to our end. Obaachan was lying on her mattress, but the light was on. She was admiring her hands again. I said, "I confessed to Mr. Laskey. I told him Thunder killed his chickens."

"What he say?" Obaachan asked. She lifted herself with a grunt. She looked worried.

"I offered him three hundred dollars, and he was so nice, he only took a hundred!"

"Not nice. He lie. Nobody pay him that much for chicken. But that stupid thing you did."

*What?* "I thought you wanted me to confess!"

"I did. But sometimes you have to do something stupid to do right thing. But right thing more important than stupid." She lay back down.

"Are you proud of me?"

Obaachan thought about that. "You did many stupid thing in a row, but I not ashamed anymore. *Oyasumi.*"

"*Oyasuminasai.*" I got in bed feeling ridiculously lighthearted. I felt like I had saved the world or something. On a whim I untucked my sheet and put my pillow on the south end of the bed. Maybe I'd have even better luck tomorrow.

# CHAPTER ELEVEN

Obaachan let me sleep in the next morning. It turned out that Jaz had the flu, and Obaachan was worried I might get sick as well, so she didn't wake me up. It was weird—one day she would scold me constantly, and the next day she'd worry I might be sick. But I was fine. It was your basic harvest day—long and quiet, with the whole crew out in the fields. I didn't see Robbie all day, so I just wandered around alone, did some homework, and helped out in the kitchen.

That night after dinner Mr. Parker said he wanted to talk about some things. Dozens and dozens of moths flitted around us. Mr. Parker offered everyone a Coke from the cooler, but Jaz and I couldn't drink any because Obaachan said bubbly things make little explosions inside of children, which can kill you eventually. If that was true, wouldn't there be a lot fewer kids around? Robbie, who'd ridden out on a dirt bike, was on his second Coke and nothing seemed to be exploding in him. Jaz was sitting with a goofy half smile. He was still sick, but he'd felt like getting out of the camper.

I scooted next to Jiichan. "How is work going?" I asked him.

"Take longer than expected. Land look flat, but bumpy underneath. My combine no have autocontour."

"Do you get tired working so late?"

"Not so bad, kind of addictive. Like in arcade when you and Jaz play game and not want to stop," Jiichan said. His eyes went glassy for a moment, then came to life again. "Big farm. Many work still to do."

Mr. Parker gave me a sharp look, so I stopped asking Jiichan questions. Mr. Parker rubbed at his scalp with the tips of his fingers. "So here's the scoop," he said, staring at the ground a moment, then glancing at his wife. He finished rubbing his scalp before continuing. "We're definitely going to have to split up. Rain's expected here, but some of us need to head to Oklahoma because rain's expected even sooner there." He sighed. "Yesterday the weather report said the rain was due early next week. Now they're saying the weekend." He looked around at everyone. "So here's what we'll do. We'll all work late tonight and tomorrow, but then Wednesday at first light, Mick, Toshiro, and Toshiro's family will head out for the Franklins' farm in Oklahoma. Larry and Rory will go along with some of the equipment, then return here. Sean and Bill will stay here in Texas."

Crud. The way we were splitting up, I probably wouldn't see Robbie for *days*. Seeing him was the highlight of my harvesting existence. Right then he was sitting and looking toward the fields, one of his legs impatiently shaking up and down.

Mick stood up, placing his hands on his waist, and leaned backward. Then everyone else stood up and stretched, like they were getting ready for a yoga class or something. The workers headed back out without a word. Robbie whispered to me, "Meet me at my place." He rode off. Jaz studied me, and I realized my mouth was a big O.

Jaz's head was lolling toward his shoulder, but he wasn't too sick to say, "I think a mosquito flew into your mouth."

But I just laughed. "You okay?" I asked.

"I wish I didn't have to move ever again." I'd noticed that he'd eaten a bit. He heaved a couple of times as if he might throw up. I placed my arms under his and helped him stand. We drove to the camper with him leaning heavily against me.

Once inside our bedroom, Jaz said, "I can't climb up there," and collapsed onto Jiichan's lower bunk.

I hurried into the kitchen to clean up dinner dishes. I wanted to get to Robbie's place. Someone kicked the door, and when I opened it, Obaachan was standing there with a handful of dishes. I held the door for her, and then went out and picked up pots and pans. The combines were already back at work. Close up, the sound was always thunderous—each of the machines we were using weighed more than thirty thousand pounds, and that was bound to make some noise. But actually, inside the cab of a combine was not as noisy as you'd expect. I watched as the machines moved side by side across the field. I heard the door open behind me, and Obaachan stepped down from the camper.

She looked off at the horizon and muttered, "Too much work for old man," and I knew she was worried about Jiichan.

"He said it's addictive," I said.

"What that?"

"It's like when you take a drug and can't stop."

"Fields are drugs?"

"I guess."

She nodded sagely. "He like working."

I was wired from thinking about going to see Robbie. Obaachan got on her hands and knees. "Do you want some aspirin?" I asked.

"Errrr," Obaachan said, her head upside down. "I way beyond aspirin. Need something from doctor."

"Do you want me to help you to bed?"

"No, this best for now."

I went back into the kitchen, thinking how even though that conversation had been short, it

173

was about the most civil one I remembered having with my grandmother. I worked as quickly as I could to get the dishes washed and the kitchen cleaned up. But I had to wipe the counters really carefully because if even the slightest spot was left, I would get a lecture from Obaachan.

"Who touched my LEGO creation?!"

I whipped around, and Jaz, looking sick, was holding up his LEGO building and staring at me.

"I accidentally bumped it, but I didn't see anything break," I said.

"I knew it! You made the cat fall off the tree! You could have just told me!"

He held out the building as if he were thinking about dropping it to the ground. He'd dropped a plate of spaghetti to the ground twice in the last year when he was mad at me. Now he stood there with his arms out for a full minute. Then he pressed his lips together and walked away instead.

By the time I finished all my chores, Obaachan had moved to her bed. She and Jaz seemed to be fast asleep. I couldn't believe my luck. I was going to sleep facing south the rest of my life.

It was nine thirty—not too late, I hoped, to go see Robbie. I went into the bathroom and remade my braids and splashed water on my face. I went to the kitchen and cut a beet in half and then touched it to my lips to make them red.

At the Parkers' camper I knocked on the door, starting to feel a little nauseous from nerves.

When Robbie opened the door, he was in his pajamas. He seemed surprised to see me. "I thought you weren't coming," he said, yawning. "Come on in." We sat on a little couch, our bodies touching. "Awww, man, harvest season is hard work."

"Really," I said. Another brilliant response. I tried to do better. "I wish I could just hang around with my friends all summer instead."

"Yeah," he said distractedly. Then he casually reached his arm around my shoulder. Ack! I just about had heart failure. "You have cool hair."

"Thank you." I could hardly get the words out because I was so nervous.

"Your grandparents seem nice," he said. "Do they ever get really mad at you?" Robbie changed the subject a lot. He also seemed to never stop shaking one of his legs, as if he were impatient to get somewhere else.

"Umm," I said. I realized that as much as Obaachan and I disagreed, she never seemed *really* mad at me. I don't know why she acted the way she acted. But it wasn't really anger. "Not so much," I answered. "I mean, only when I fight with my brother. He has some . . . problems. I mean, one problem, which is his really bad temper. He gets furious and tries to hurt himself. But it's not his fault." That was a long paragraph, and I felt really pleased with myself.

"Whose fault is it?"

I didn't really believe it was my parents' fault. I didn't know whose fault it was.

"Sometimes it's mine," I said. At least that was what my mother once said when she was mad at me. "My mother says I need to be gentle with him."

"I like to be gentle," Robbie said, and he suddenly leaned over and kissed me. I was so shocked, I made a little noise. I didn't know what to do with my lips. Should I just make them into a kissing shape and not move them? And if I did move them, what exactly should I do? One thing

I knew was not to hold them hard like the Rock of Gibraltar.

As I was thinking all this, Robbie suddenly stopped. "I have to get to bed because I need to get up early and clean the combines." He yawned again. "I'll kiss you again tomorrow," he added, almost as if he was bored. I wondered if boys generally let you know ahead of time that they're going to kiss you. "I'll teach you how."

Oh no! That meant I hadn't done it right. On the other hand—yay! He was going to kiss me again!

He stood up and walked with me to the door. "See ya," he said, and closed the door.

I stood there, my hands shaking when I held them out in front of me. "These are my hands," I said, just to ground myself. "This is me."

I couldn't move. I turned to stare at his door and replay the last few minutes in my head. Sometimes my friends and I talked about kissing, but so far, it had only been talk. Still, around the time I was leaving, the girls and boys in my class had started to notice one another in a new way. I wondered if this was part of the change my mother said was coming. Maybe I didn't have to spend the summer at home to experience this change. If I had a phone, I could call Melody and talk to her. I made a mental note to sneak out with Obaachan's cell phone one day.

When I got back to our camper, I expected to be lectured by Obaachan for being gone, but my luck was still holding because she was still asleep. Jaz was awake, though. He didn't seem mad anymore. He never stayed mad for long. I went to the bathroom and put on a long T-shirt. When I got to the bedroom, I felt my way through the dark.

"Where were you?" Jaz asked softly.

"Robbie's," I answered quietly.

"Does he like you? Did he kiss you?"

I swear, sometimes I thought he had ESP that he'd inherited from our grandmother.

"MYOB," I told him. But I felt giddy.

"I'll take that as a yes. I think it would make me throw up to kiss you." He didn't say that in a mean way. He was just stating a fact.

"That's because you're my brother. It could be I did kiss him, but I'm not going to tell *you*.

And don't talk so loud—I don't want Obaachan to wake up."

"Summer? Seriously."

"What?"

"What will happen when I grow up?" he said.

"What do you mean?"

"Will I have friends? Will I have a job? Am I too much of a weirdo?"

I paused. Once in a while he'd just abruptly ask me questions like these. It all revolved around the fact that he didn't have friends. For a moment I couldn't think of a thing to say. Then he said, "I'm sad."

Ohhh. I felt a rush of love for my brother. "Your life won't be sad," I said. "I'm positive."

I saw a luna moth the size of my hand on the window. I couldn't tell if it was inside or outside. It was so graceful, more like an exotic leaf than an insect. Luna moths did not feed because they had no mouths, so the one I was looking at would be dead soon. What a crazy world!

"Why do you think that?" Jaz asked.

I couldn't really help him much because I had never been a grown-up, so I didn't know what it would be like. Finally, I said, "Sometimes you'll be happy and sometimes you'll be sad, just like anyone."

"But I'll be more sad than happy, won't I? Just like now."

Then I had a brainstorm. "With you, it won't matter if you're happy or sad. You'll just be intense, like you are now, and then your life will be perfect."

He thought that over. "I'll accept that for now."

What was that supposed to mean? Sometimes he seemed like a complicated adult instead of a little boy. I thought about it some more. He was kind of unplaceable, actually, neither young nor old.

I climbed up to my second-level bunk and Thunder leapt up with me.

Obaachan said, "I never go to sleep."

"What?" I nearly tumbled off the mattress.

"I never go to sleep. I no need."

She was trying to tell me she had heard the whole conversation. So be it. I fell asleep.

I think we all slept lightly until Jiichan came in. I heard the squeak of his feet on the kitchen linoleum, and that small noise woke me. I didn't know what time it was. "Hi, Jiichan," Jaz and I both said.

"You two up still?"

"I was thinking about life," Jaz said. "I'm in your bed."

It was very dark, but I heard the sound of Jiichan climbing into the other second-level bed without changing. "I tell you a story about life, and then you go to sleep. When I live in Wakayama-ken, I get lost. I walk, but I think of school instead of think of walk. Then I don't know where I am. Everywhere is mandarin orange farm. Which way to go? It starting to be night. I see stars. I finally walk to farmhouse. I knock on door. Biggest man I ever see answer door. Mean face. I think he want to eat me, and I run away. I spend night outside, sleeping with oranges. My parents find me next day. They say school number one important, but even number one you don't have to think of all the time. When you walk, think of walk. *Oyasumi*."

"*Oyasuminasai*, Jiichan."

# CHAPTER TWELVE

The next afternoon the temperature hit 103 degrees. It was also grocery shopping day, but Obaachan said I had to stay home to study and also to take care of my brother. Jaz didn't have to do anything at all because he was still sick. But he was bored, so I read him *A Separate Peace*.

"Summer, do you have any other books? This is the most boring book ever written."

"I have two books about girls."

"Is that it?"

"Yep."

"Okay, keep reading."

I kept reading, listening to my gravelly voice.

Maybe someday I could do voice-overs for commercials. That's what I was thinking about when I realized Jaz had fallen asleep.

We were cooking chili for dinner. I had cleaned and soaked the kidney beans overnight, so I took them out of the fridge. I poured the beans into a big pot and brought them to a boil, then turned them down to a simmer. Even with the air-conditioning, sweat beaded on my face. Mrs. Parker had brought a pressure cooker, but Obaachan didn't want to use it because she was afraid it might explode. "Pressure most powerful force in world," she had said. Then she'd seemed to be in an argument with herself: "Of course, nuclear bomb powerful too. But pressure make things blow up, so that just as bad. I think about this and get back to you."

The beans had to simmer until they were soft. Every so often, I would stir them and check to see if they were ready.

It was kind of relaxing while Obaachan was at the store. I spent my time reading an article that Jiichan had given Jaz and me copies of. He did that sometimes when he happened across something interesting he'd read. The article was called "Opinions and Social Pressure," and it was dated 1955, first published in *Scientific American*.

"Opinions and Social Pressure" was kind of hard to understand, but not as hard as you might think. It was pretty straightforward and didn't use a lot of big words. Basically, it was about research on peer pressure and showed how this kind of pressure could literally change what people saw with their own eyes. They would think a long line on a large white card was short and a short line was long, just because everyone else said so. And once you started down the road of giving in to peer pressure, you couldn't escape. The research showed this. You might never know what you saw with your own eyes.

I knew Jiichan was making us read this article so we wouldn't give in to peer pressure. Peer pressure was a big fear of his. And, strangely enough, Jiichan seemed more worried about Jaz than about me. I thought this was odd since Jaz was so different that he would always be completely out of step with the other kids in his class. He could never give in to peer pressure, because he could only be himself. But Jiichan suspected Jaz was more vulnerable, because having a friend made him so happy that he would start to see the world the way the friend told him to if that was the best way to keep this friend.

Obaachan returned from the store in an hour and a half and went straight to our room. I knew she wanted to be with Jaz because he was sick. I chopped the onions and measured out all the ingredients. The onions made me cry like crazy. Supposedly, Monsanto, a huge agricultural bio-technology company, was developing an onion that wouldn't make you cry when you chopped it. Jiichan had read this in the newspaper and was so upset that Monsanto would change onions into something that weren't exactly onions any-more that he wrote about twenty different letters to various people and organizations, protesting Monsanto. He got back twenty polite letters that didn't really commit to one thing or another, then thanked him for his interest.

I cooked and crumbled the ground beef and threw all the ingredients into a giant pot, where it had to simmer for an hour and a half more with occasional stirring. Making chili was a major time commitment.

Because Robbie had kissed me last night, I wanted to get dressed up for dinner, so I changed into the only skirt I'd brought, which was a couple of inches above my knees and the color of the sky. Just before eight p.m., we drove into the field and set up dinner. Rory plunked onto a canvas chair and leaned his head back. "I don't know why, but I'm just banjaxed today."

"Ah, quit acting the maggot," Mick shot back.

"I'm serious. I hope that little fella didn't give me his germs."

Jaz was lying in the pickup—he'd wanted to get out of the camper for a while.

"Trying to get yerself a holiday?" Mick asked.

Robbie walked over to the chili pot and filled his bowl. He was totally ignoring me. After the rest of the crew got their food, it was silent for a few minutes as everyone ate. Then Mick muttered, "A bit salty, isn't it?" That made me feel exhausted, like no matter what I did, it wouldn't be good enough.

Mrs. Parker said, "Yes, a bit."

I wished someone would say it was delicious. It was kind of disheartening to spend all afternoon making chili and then see everyone scarf it up in eight minutes and call it too salty.

Anyway. Maybe everyone was eating quickly because this was the last chance to work with the whole crew before some of us headed to Oklahoma. Jiichan started flossing his teeth.

Mrs. Parker looked aghast. "I don't think that's really hygienic, Toshiro."

He looked up. "Excuse me?"

"Jiichan, she wants you to stop flossing in front of everyone," I explained.

"Oh, oh, my dentist tell me to floss as much as I can. But I stop now." He seemed genuinely surprised. He looked down at his chili, as if he didn't know how it had gotten in front of him. Then he stood up and wavered a moment, the chili spilling to the ground. Mr. Parker and I jumped up to steady him. He closed his eyes and leaned against me.

Mr. Parker pushed me away and sat Jiichan in his chair. "What is it?" he asked.

"I feel sick for a minute, but I okay now." His face did have a pasty cast to it.

Obaachan got up and put her palm on his forehead. "Maybe he sick from Jaz," she said. "His forehead very hot." As if on cue, Jaz came out of the pickup just then and joined us in the dining area.

"I don't want you working any more tonight," Mrs. Parker decided.

"We need him working. We need to get as much work as possible done tonight," Mr. Parker retorted.

"I hard worker," Jiichan piped up. "I can work."

"I know you're a hard worker," Mr. Parker said. "That's why I want you out there."

Mrs. Parker looked doubtfully at Jiichan, then said more decisively, "It's out of the question. Look at the man. His skin is practically gray."

Jaz blurted out, "Summer can drive a combine. My dad taught her. Even I can drive a tractor, except I'm sick now." He collapsed into Mick's lap, smiling strangely. My heart fluttered with fear. It was true I had driven under field conditions twice at the Hillbinkses' farm near our house. And their combine—though a different model than the Parkers had rented—was also a John Deere. But I hadn't gone past one mile an hour and my dad had been there the whole time. I doubted I was good enough to go out on my own. I gave Jaz the stink-eye. He jolted out of Mick's lap and staggered back to the pickup.

"I can't do it!" I said. "What if I mess up?"

"She no can do," Obaachan said. "I forbid. She make mistake. She maybe break combine. Maybe hit another combine and break two at same time. Then her mother and father be in debt for rest of life."

"How much experience do you have?" Mrs. Parker asked, looking at me with interest.

"Five hours," I answered.

"Has everyone lost their minds? We can't have a twelve-year-old girl driving a combine!" Mr. Parker said. He turned to Jiichan. "You're sure you can't work?"

"Absolutely not!" Mrs. Parker exclaimed.

"Honey, let me talk to the man."

"I can work," Jiichan said. "I hard worker."

"Absolutely not!" Mrs. Parker exclaimed again.

She turned to Mr. Parker. They stared at each other for three full seconds.

Suddenly, Mr. Parker's shoulders drooped and he gave up, mumbling, "Happy wife, happy life."

The others scattered after our quick meal, heading back to work and casting worried glances at my grandfather as they left.

"You go lie down," Obaachan told him. Then, even though Jiichan hadn't uttered a word, she said, "Why you want to argue with me?"

"I don't feel like lie down."

"I know you since you seventeen year old. I knew you going to argue with me," Obaachan said.

"I knew you going to say that," Jiichan retorted. "You want to argue about everything. You argue more than me."

"That not true. You argue the most."

Then they spent the next couple of minutes arguing about arguing. In the end, Jiichan relented and got into the passenger seat.

"I need to work," he said petulantly. But he closed his eyes and said, "Ahhh," as if it felt really good to slump down.

After Obaachan and I got Jaz and Jiichan into bed, Obaachan began washing dishes. I dried. "By the way, I decide. Pressure most powerful force on Earth."

I didn't answer. When the kitchen was clean, I went outside with a flashlight to walk Thunder before confining him for the night. The field looked barren, like a bomb had been dropped. It was the opposite of the flowing field the workers were cutting. I thought about our skimpy savings and wondered if they would deduct some of Jiichan's salary because he couldn't work tonight. And worse yet, what if we got fired?

Thunder galloped through the cut field. He flushed out a rabbit and took off in pursuit. They were both so fast. I stood still to admire Thunder's muscular black body bounding in the moonlight. He caught the rabbit in his mouth and shook it dead. Back home when he did that, we ate the rabbit meat. Dogs killed rabbits, mosquitoes killed people, and people killed just about anything. But I really thought we all had good souls. That was so deep, I made a mental note of it.

"Thunder!" I called out. He tore back across the field and barreled into me with his dead, bloody rabbit. I took the rabbit inside, where Obaachan was reading a Japanese magazine. "Look what Thunder caught."

"Rabbit not in Mrs. Parker's recipes. Get that out of here."

"Can I cook it for Thunder?"

Obaachan seemed to consider that. "If you clean up after."

I took out a big knife. "Is there a hammer someplace?" I asked Obaachan.

"Use that," she said, gesturing to one of the recipe books. "I do it."

So I rested the knife blade on the rabbit's ankles, and Obaachan pounded down on the blade, snapping the back feet off. We did that with the front feet and the tail as well. Finally, we did the head. Starting at the ankle, I yanked the rabbit's skin off. Thunder was whining impatiently next to me. I gutted and rinsed the rabbit, saving the liver. Then I started boiling the meat with carrots and celery.

Obaachan went to check on Jiichan and Jaz.

We'd turned down the air conditioner to save energy for the Parkers. But with the stove back on, sweat started to drip down my face and chest. I washed my hands and stepped outside. It didn't feel much better out there, but at least it was windy. The uncut wheat looked like a flying carpet in the distance.

I stared for a moment at the Parkers' camper. I decided to go say hi to Robbie, then I decided not to because it was being too forward and he'd been ignoring me. Then I decided to do it after all. I knocked, and Robbie answered. Right behind him was Mr. Laskey's pretty daughter. I stared at her for a moment. I was so surprised that for a second it was like my whole brain was empty. Then I blurted out to her, "What are you doing here?"

Robbie turned to her and said, "Her grandfather is a combine driver for us." And from the way he said it, I could tell he meant that I wasn't important, and neither was my family. I remembered I still had my apron on. I looked down and saw blood and guts on it. Anger and sadness washed over me at the same time, and I was torn between wanting to cry and wanting to shout at him.

Instead, I said calmly, "You didn't seem bothered by that when you kissed me." He looked truly surprised, and I felt a surge of triumph.

I walked away, making sure to hold my head high. Jaz was sitting by himself under our "porch" light, his head lolling to the side. "What's that?" he asked me.

"What's what? I'm in a bad mood, so don't bother me. What are you doing up?"

"There's something on your forehead."

I wiped at my forehead and found a piece of rabbit guts. That meant I'd had it on my forehead when I went to see Robbie. Wasn't that wonderful? "Mind your own business!"

"I've said it before and I'll say it again: What did I do?" Jaz scratched at his face, then suddenly fell to his knees and started pounding his head on the ground. I grabbed him from behind, enveloping his arms. He was too sick to put up much of a fight, and in a moment he calmed down. Sometimes he did that as a trick, so that I would let go and he could pound his forehead some more. I took a chance and released him. We were both dripping sweat. He lay out on the ground like Obaachan does, then gagged.

"If you're going to throw up, maybe you should sit up so you don't choke," I said. "Why are you even out of bed?"

"I don't know. I'm sick of being inside. I'm just going to lie here and maybe go to sleep."

"You can't sleep out here."

"Will you carry me inside?"

"I can help you, but I can't lift you."

"Then I'm going to lie here." He closed his eyes and really did seem to be asleep.

I sat on the steps and leaned my head back against the door for a long time. I felt like I didn't understand a single thing in the whole world. I didn't understand a single person. I didn't even understand myself.

I went inside and took Obaachan's cell phone from her purse. Then I went back outside, away from Jaz, and dialed Melody. One of the combines was driving in for some reason.

"Hi, Mel."

"Summer! I was just thinking about you. Mr.

Lerner had a family emergency so we have a substitute for the rest of the year, and he gives *so* much homework and he's *so* mean. You're lucky you're not here."

"Mel, I kissed a boy." I spoke urgently but also quietly enough that Jaz couldn't hear me.

"What?! Who?"

"A boy named Robbie Parker. He's the son of the people we're working for. I had a crush on him, and then he must have liked me too because he kissed me."

"That's amazing!"

"No, now he likes the girl who lives at the farm here, and he kind of insulted my grandfather."

"Oh, that's terrible. What a jerk!"

"And I have to see him all the time for the whole rest of the harvest season. What should I do?"

"Maybe he'll apologize to you."

"Nobody can insult my grandfather. I don't even like him anymore."

Then the camper door started opening, and I slipped the phone into my pocket.

Obaachan stepped out. "Don't ever leave stove on when you go out. What I just say?"

"Don't ever leave the stove on when I go out," Jaz and I both recited.

The combine that had been heading in finally reached the edge of the wheat field and pulled to a stop. Mrs. Parker climbed down and headed over.

"I was worried about Toshiro and wanted to check on him," she said. She glanced at Jaz. "Why is he on the ground?" She cocked her head. "And what is that sound?" It was Mel's little voice talking to me from my apron pocket.

"My husband sleeping already," Obaachan said.

"Do you think we need a doctor?"

"No doctor. Doctor give you pill and make you drug addict. He get better. Jaz stay sick a long time, but Toshiro never sick long time in his life."

Mrs. Parker looked thoughtful. "Well, all right, if you think he'll be fine." She glanced at Jaz again. "You can't leave him there."

"He's too heavy for me to carry, and he refused to get up unless I carry him," I explained.

"Well, that's a problem easily solved," Mrs. Parker said. She knelt down and, with a huge grunt, pulled Jaz over her shoulder, as if he weighed twenty pounds instead of eighty.

Then she said, "There is that noise again!" Then the noise stopped, and I knew that Mel had hung up.

I held the door open as Mrs. Parker climbed up the three stairs into the camper, grunting all the way. She tried to lay Jaz in a bottom bunk, but she missed and got only one side of his body onto the mattress. His other side, with nothing to support it, pulled him down. He plopped to the floor. "Ahh," he groaned. "Mrs. Parker, please don't ever do that again."

"I'm so sorry, Jaz."

Jaz slowly pushed himself up and fell into bed.

"Now all of you get some rest. I can't be worrying about everyone while I'm driving," she said crisply.

I liked Mrs. Parker. I mean, she was a pain in the neck, but at the same time I knew she was a pain in the neck only because she cared about all of us. I followed her outside. I had a question that I would ordinarily ask my mother. But since Mom wasn't around, I thought I should ask Mrs. Parker. When we reached her combine, she turned to me. "What is it, Summer?"

"Mrs. Parker?"

"Yes?"

"Have you ever felt humiliated and proud at the same time?" I blurted out.

"It's the human condition, sweetie," she said in her no-nonsense voice. "Now you get some rest. It's late." She climbed up her combine.

I realized how exhausted I was. Being humiliated and then getting mad had done me in. I went inside, returned Obaachan's cell phone, and lay down in my bunk, together with my sick, sleeping family, where I felt safe.

# CHAPTER THIRTEEN

The chirp of crickets accompanied the soft sounds of country music—the music a little scratchy from the cheap radio, the chirping strong and clear and seemingly coming from everywhere in the world all at once. In the dim morning I could see Robbie inside the cab of a combine, cleaning the windows. It was six a.m. Jiichan and Mick each loaded a combine onto a trailer attached to a semi. The music was coming

from one of the big rigs, with Mr. Dark sitting in the cab waiting for everyone to load up.

This is what our group was bringing to Oklahoma:

1. Big rig hauling combine and grain trailer
2. Big rig hauling combine
3. Pickup hauling header
4. Pickup hauling header

Jiichan and Mick would each drive a big rig. Rory and Mr. Dark would ride together in one of the pickups. Obaachan would drive the other pickup. Then Rory would drive one of the pickups back to Texas, and Mr. Dark would drive one of the big rigs back. Or something like that. It all made my head spin.

Once we got to the Franklin place and started cutting, Jiichan and Mick would dump directly into the grain trailer instead of into a grain cart.

Then Obaachan would drive the semi, with the grain trailer attached, to and from an elevator. She'd gotten her commercial driver's license a couple of years earlier, so she was allowed.

As we set out around six thirty, Jiichan was still sick, but he was trying hard to pretend he was fine. He'd told Mrs. Parker that he and Obaachan were feeling well. Maybe that was the wrong thing to say, because now Obaachan had to drive the pickup to Oklahoma, though it would have made more sense for Mr. Dark to drive us. Mr. Dark was getting a rest because he hadn't slept well.

But since the drive wasn't long, I thought both Jiichan and Obaachan could make it. Jaz and I did *jan ken pon* to decide who had to ride with Obaachan. I lost. "Errrrr," Obaachan kept saying. She didn't talk much, just seemed absorbed in her pain.

After a while I fell asleep. When I opened my eyes, we were parked by the side of the highway. Everyone except me had gathered around Obaachan. She was lying on her back on the roadside.

"How long has my grandmother been there?" I asked, getting out of the pickup.

"About ten minutes," Mick said. "I don't know why yer grandparents came when they can barely work."

"They work just as hard as you," I said, but he didn't respond. "Obaachan, can you get up?" I asked, kneeling by her side.

She held out her hands. Jaz and I each took a hand and pulled her up. She seemed surprisingly light, even more so than usual, as if she were fading away into nothing this morning.

I was surprised to see Obaachan get in the passenger side. They must all have been talking while I slept. Now Mr. Dark would drive the semi Jiichan had been driving, and Jiichan would drive us in the pickup.

Jaz climbed into the truck after me.

We all started off again. "I tell you I drive," Obaachan said. "Stubborn old man."

"You stubborn old woman," Jiichan said. "I can drive."

"Who old? You older than me!"

"Only one month older!"

"Thirty-five days! That more than month!"

It amazed me that they could argue about

the smallest things even when they were trying to do something nice for each other. Each of
them wanted to drive in order to save the other
from having to. "They're expressing love for each
other," my dad had once said while he was watching a football game. "That's just the way they talk.
Down in front—I just missed a touchdown!"

Before I got malaria, I used to think that my
dad loved sports more than he loved me. But
then while I was sick, my whole family practically moved into my hospital room. I had a vague,
almost hallucinogenic memory of them drifting
around the room like silent ghosts. I felt like I was
alive and they were the walking dead. We were in
two different worlds. But in my world I just *knew*
how badly my father wanted me to get well. In
fact, I knew everything. I did.

"How far are we?" I asked Obaachan now.

"You need sleep" was all she said.

Then I thought of Mick and felt anger rise in
me. Jiichan happened to have gotten sick, but
otherwise, he worked just as much and just as
hard as Mick. And Obaachan and I cooked for
everyone every day. We were all doing good jobs,

and he had no right to say what he'd said. I didn't like Mick at all.

I turned my head toward the window, my mind filled with evil thoughts about Mick. I wished he would fall out of the truck and get run over by another truck. Then I felt guilty for thinking that. But you know how it is. You can't stop yourself from thinking something. At least, that's what I believed. My parents agreed with me, but my grandparents didn't. In fact, all that meditating I did was supposed to help me think nicer thoughts. Sometimes it was hard, though.

Maybe that was why I kept thinking about *A Separate Peace*. Gene was jealous of Finny, and then one day he acted on that jealousy by shaking the branch so that Finny fell to the ground. I had decided that Gene shook the branch on purpose. I didn't want to do something horrible like that in the future. It scared me that I might have evil inside of me. That was why I never argued when Jiichan said I should try to meditate and do my breathing exercises. This would help me to open up my heart more.

I closed my eyes again.

After a long time I heard Mick on the radio saying we had reached the motel Mrs. Parker had booked for us.

"We're going to drop the machines at the farm," Mick said. "It's a bit up the road. Yukiko, why don't ya get our rooms? Tosh, ya ought to come to the farm after ya drop yer family off."

Jiichan pulled into a gravel lot below a sign reading WHEATLAND MOTEL. A small group of people were just leaving the motel. They were probably wheaties like us. I could tell somehow.

I stayed in the pickup because I had just decided to follow Jiichan around all day to make sure he was okay. Jaz got out with Obaachan and cried loudly into the wind, "For I am the great LEGO builder Jaz Miyamoto! I come to conquer your state!" When we reached the farm, Rory was already unloading a combine. Then he got in a semi without a word and set off for Texas again. Mr. Dark climbed into a pickup and drove off. I had no idea how everyone was operating on so little sleep.

Jiichan put a weird trying-to-appear-fine grin on his face. Mick cut a swath of wheat with a combine, then climbed into the bin with a moisture meter. "Too moist," he called out. We hopped back into the pickup and returned to the motel to check in and sleep while the wheat dried.

Obaachan and Jaz were sitting on a bench outside the office. She got up when she saw us and handed Mick his keycard. "Let's meet in two hours, then I'll check the moisture again," Mick said.

Jiichan nodded. He usually walked with perfect posture, but now his shoulders slumped. I held on to his hand as we walked to our room. Obaachan and Jiichan immediately got into bed, so Jaz and I unloaded the pickup. We'd brought bottles of water, two thermoses of coffee, and one suitcase apiece. We weren't expecting to be here very long.

It seemed as if I had just fallen asleep when I heard knocking. I staggered sleepily to the door. When I opened up, Mick stood there looking exhausted, looking, in fact, a lot like my family.

"The wheat's ready," he said. "Mr. Franklin called. He's waiting at the farmhouse for us." He held up a thermos. "I don't know how Americans drink so much coffee. Awful stuff, but it does wake a man up."

"Do you want to wait in here?" I asked him. "We'll just be a few minutes."

"I'll wait outside."

Obaachan was already up and dressed in fresh clothes. She was the Incredible Sleepless Woman. She was listening to music on an MP3 player. She liked Bruce Springsteen. Go figure. It was pretty funny when she cried out lyrics like "Take a knife and cut this pain from my heart!" She took one of the thermoses and filled the cap with coffee. "Tosh," she said. "Sorry, very sorry, but you have work now."

Jiichan opened his eyes but didn't move. He finally sat up. "This worst moment of my life," he said before getting out of bed. I felt so bad for him. We had all gone to sleep fully dressed. He went to use the bathroom before walking out without changing. Obaachan and I followed him. She would need to take the pickup back and forth from the motel to the big rig as she alternately went to the elevator and relaxed in the motel. I let Thunder stay in the motel because I didn't want any trouble.

Several acres' length away, we approached

a farmhouse. There was a man sitting on the porch, a shotgun on his lap. The only reason to have a shotgun was to hunt, and I was pretty sure he wasn't doing any hunting, sitting on the porch. Obaachan waited in the pickup.

The man stood up. "Parker Harvesting?"

"We are," Mick said. He put out his hand. "I be Mick. This be Toshiro."

"I never seen a Chinese wheatie before," the farmer said, eyeing Jiichan.

"Japanese," I piped up extra politely when Jiichan or Mick didn't correct him. I don't know why, but I felt like I had to use my best manners with people who didn't deal with many Asians. I felt like I was representing the whole Asian race. The farmer looked at me closely and didn't move his gaze. "You just stuck your finger into an electric socket?" he said. I remembered my hair. Then he smiled. I smiled back.

"You Irish?" he said to Mick.

"I am."

"Seen those before. We had two from South Africa last year."

"Did ya, then?" Mick said.

The farmer checked his watch. "You're sure it's ready?"

"I am."

"You're looking a little ragged. Hope you have enough energy to do this job."

"We do," Mick said.

Jiichan came to life. "We hard worker."

"Well, have at it. I got almost fifteen hundred acres here, and it's supposed to rain this weekend. It's gonna be close. I figure you're each gonna have to cut close to twenty acres an hour."

"We'll be getting started, then," Mick said.

The farmer returned to his seat. I could feel his eyes on us as we headed back to the pickup. They felt like heat on my back. Farmers could be very intense people during harvest.

"What did he have a gun for?" I asked when we were out of hearing distance.

"Many crazy people in America. I don't know why," Jiichan answered.

I waved to Obaachan and she drove off. "You don't know why there are so many crazy people in America, or you don't know why he had a gun?"

I asked. "Oh, no! I forgot my DEET." I felt for a moment that I couldn't breathe.

"Go back to motel," Jiichan told me.

"Will someone drive me back there in the big rig?" I implored. "Please? I want to ride with Jiichan."

Mick appraised me with a harsh face. We were all already perspiring. I wiped my arm across my face and then wiped my arm on my shorts.

"Ya're going to have to walk. We're on a deadline," Mick replied.

I really disliked that man, even if he was right.

I scanned the farm. The field sloped gently on the south side. It looked like windblown sand beneath the bright sky.

I had to decide whether I should ride with Jiichan or walk back to the motel to get my DEET. Jiichan climbed up the combine, and I followed. "Are you sure you can do this?" I asked him.

He stared straight ahead, his lips pressed together. "I hard worker."

"I know you are, but you're sick."

Instead of replying, he pushed the key into the ignition and blew the horn twice, which you were always supposed to do before you moved a combine, to warn anyone standing around to get out of the way.

The passenger seat was really uncomfortable, so I folded my legs on the chair. The Parkers made sure every combine had a flashlight, a banana for potassium, and a bottle of water at all times. I held the banana up to Jiichan, and he shook his head. He turned on the air-conditioning and closed his eyes as the cold air washed over us.

Every time I'd ever climbed into a combine, I felt small. It was like riding on a small house. Jiichan honked the horn twice again. The machine was trembling. He pulled to the side of where Mick had already begun cutting. He had left us a strip of uncut wheat at the edge of the field.

When I turned back to Jiichan, he was pushing the throttle lever to five miles an hour. I thought about Robbie. If he liked that Laskey girl better than me, then that was the way it was. But why did he have to say what he said the way he said it? Then my mind wandered back to mosquitoes. They'd been around for thirty million years. I had read once that supposedly if you put all the ants in the world together, they would weigh more than all the humans in the world. I wondered if that was also true of mosquitoes. My father said that was the problem with me—I wondered too much and filled my head with nonsense about mosquitoes. He thought that was because having malaria hurt not only my body but also my mind, and it might take a long time for my mind to heal. If I didn't meditate, maybe my mind would never heal, Jiichan had added.

I remembered again how my dog Shika had known she was about to die. When I had malaria, I could think, but it was like I was thinking with a different brain than my normal brain. And then something happened—the medicine defeated the parasites, I guess. So I didn't die. And then when I was completely well, I was a different kid—a kid who knew I could die. Before that, I never thought about dying at all.

I looked up and saw that Mick was driving by our side. I waved at him, but he didn't wave back.

"Funny feeling," Jiichan said out of the blue.

"What?"

"Funny feeling," he said again. I waited for an explanation, but none came. Then a minute later he put the combine into idle. He seemed to be deep in thought.

"I may need break," he said.

For a second I didn't know if he meant "break" or "brake."

"Feeling funny."

"What do you need?" I asked, suddenly alert.

"I just need to sit and think."

The radio came to life. "Everything all right, then?" Mick asked.

Jiichan picked up the speaker. "Everything fine. I just thinking."

"Thinking, ya said?"

"Yes, I need thinking."

Mick didn't reply, and Jiichan engaged the combine again. We hit a patch of weeds. I could smell them being cut up and shot out the back, and I could hear the combine grumble as the weeds went through the machinery.

I looked at Jiichan's gloomy face. He was a happy man. I had rarely seen him so gloomy. It made me want to cry. Jiichan seemed to be weighing his options. But he didn't speak again.

# CHAPTER FOURTEEN

A few hours later Obaachan, Jaz, and Thunder rode into the field in the pickup. Obaachan's handbag was full of vending machine goodies: trail mix, candy bars, Fritos, water, and other drinks. "Now, there's a nutritious meal," Mick said, biting into a Snickers. Jiichan drank some Gatorade, but he said he didn't feel like eating. I ate some stale trail mix.

Once we were ready to return to work, Obaachan asked, "How you feel, old man?"

Jiichan swatted at the air in annoyance.

Obaachan drove off to take the cut grain to the elevator. Thunder howled out the window. Sometimes he did that when we were separated.

Jiichan and I climbed back into the combine, and he drove without comment. Things were going smoothly except that sometimes Jiichan's jaw was slack and his head tilted slightly. I knew he would like nothing better than to climb into bed. It was around five when we took our next break, and I could still feel the warm air on my face. We stood together in the middle of the field, the wind blowing hard around us. Jiichan reached for the sky and leaned back with his eyes closed. I focused on the air, searching for mosquitoes. But there were none.

After a few minutes we returned to the combine. My grandfather started the engine, honked twice, and then sat there for at least a full minute. Then he said, "I no can drive no more." He sunk down in his seat. "Turn off."

"Me?" I leaned over and carefully took hold of a lever. I pulled the lever back into middle position. I saw out the glass that Mick was driving on. The farmer's fields were long and somewhat narrow.

"Your *obaachan* drive when her neck hurt, I should drive when I sick. But she stronger than me. Tell Mick I need quit now. Cannot do more."

I gingerly picked up the radio. "My grandfather is finished."

"Is he all right, then?"

"I don't know," I replied honestly.

"You drive back to pickup," Jiichan said. "I no can. Then you drive me in pickup to motel."

Doubt fluttered through me. "But the pickup is a stick shift," I said. "I don't think I can drive it." In Kansas you could get your learner's permit at age fourteen. So I'd practiced driving with my father, but our pickup was an automatic. I looked at the expanse of wheat still uncut. I looked at the sky, which was getting overcast. I hoped the rains didn't come early. I looked at Jiichan.

"Then drive me in combine to motel," he said.

My heart was pounding as I climbed out onto the platform, Jiichan following. Then we got back into the combine, me first, sitting behind the steering wheel, him in the passenger seat. I felt very small. I suddenly knew what it must feel like to be a mouse. I took the combine out of idle and slowly headed across the field toward the pickup. I checked Mick's combine through the side mirror.

The land here was more terraced than the land on the Laskey farm. This made the going slower. There was no way one combine could cut all the wheat that was here in only a few days. Even though it was a small farm, right then it seemed like the biggest farm in the world. The combine shook as I rolled into a trench hidden beneath the remnants of cut wheat. That shook me up, and I had to go into idle again.

Jiichan had closed his eyes. "Jiichan?" I said, but he didn't answer. When we reached the pickup, I turned off the combine and just sat there. With Jiichan asleep, I wasn't sure what to do. On the farm across the street, I saw someone else's combines driving through the wheat fields. I wondered if we would have to offer our job to them in order to be finished on time. And if we did that, how much would it cost the Parkers? And would they dock our pay? I pocketed the key so nobody could steal the combine.

The radio came to life. "Is he quitting, then?"

"Yes," I answered. "He wants me to drive him to the motel in the combine."

"I'll handle it," Mick said. "Just wait there."

I sat and watched Mick bring his combine in. He climbed down the ladder, hopping down the last few rungs and hurrying over before climbing up our combine. He flung open the door and studied Jiichan, who appeared to be sleeping.

"I won't be able to get him down the ladder. Can ya wake him?" Mick asked.

"Sure." I shook Jiichan gently. That didn't work, so I leaned over and said, "Jiichan? Jiichan!" His head rolled over to the left. "Mick's here. He can take us to the motel in the pickup."

Jiichan opened his eyes. "Thank you," he said. "Thank you, Mick."

When we got back to the motel, Mick helped Jiichan into our room, where he crumpled into his bed. "Let me know if ya need anything," Mick said. "Here, write down my cell phone number."

I got a pen and wrote his number on a Wheatland Motel pad of paper. Then he was gone. I sat on the bed I was sharing with Jaz. Obaachan, Jaz, and Thunder were still at the elevator. In a minute the phone rang, startling me.

"Hello?" I said.

"It's Mr. Parker."

"Hi!"

"Is your grandfather going back to work?"

Mick must have just called him. "Uh, not exactly. I mean, not right at this moment."

"Tell him we don't have much time."

I glanced at the clock—it was almost six in the evening.

"He's going back out tonight," I lied. "He didn't get enough sleep." I just felt like I wanted to get off the phone.

"A short rest is acceptable," Mr. Parker said crisply. "But tell him to try to make it short. Can you do that? It's just a nap he needs?"

"I hope so," I said honestly.

Mr. Parker sighed, then fell silent.

"Hello?" I said.

"*Que sera, sera,*" he finally answered. I knew that song: *Whatever will be, will be. The future's not ours to see, que sera, sera.* "If he's too sick, of course he shouldn't go back out. Don't mind me. Let me know either way, if he goes back out today or doesn't. I'd like to keep all my customers happy if possible. Okay, bye."

"Bye."

I could almost feel Mr. Parker's torment pulling him every which way. *Be nice, be firm, be nice, be firm. Take care of the people, take care of the crops.*

I went outside with some homework. I looked around. I missed Thunder. A mosquito landed on my arm, and I scrambled up, screaming. A man opened the door of the office down the way. "Was that you?" he called out.

"It was nothing."

"A scream like that for nothing?"

"It was . . . a mosquito."

He just stared at me for a moment before returning to the office.

I went inside our room, took a shower, and spread DEET all over myself. My stomach hurt. If we messed up this job, how would we pay our mortgage? If we lost the house, where would we live? I took out my journal and a pen and sat on the floor, using the closed toilet as a table.

One of our essay assignments was to write about who we would like to be if we weren't ourselves. This didn't quite make sense as an assignment, because you couldn't know who you really wanted to be until you tried out life from their point of view for a while. But I attempted to do the best I could.

If I could be anyone else in the world, it would be, my grandfather. He is sixty-seven years, four months, and three days old. He is from Japan. He came here because my mother was born in the United States during a long visit he was taking with my grandmother. My mother was a preemee and they were scared, she might die the doctor said. But she did not. My grandfather is a combine driver. There are probably, maybe, approximately three thousand combine drivers working right now in America this very summer. Maybe less. That's not too many. They work hard. But I ~~wouldn't~~ would not be a good combine driver because

Suddenly, I couldn't remember if it was my new teacher or my old one who didn't like contractions. I stopped. I had an idea. I mean, it was a really big idea. It was such a big idea that my hands started shaking. I couldn't concentrate on my homework anymore. The front door opened, startling me. I stepped into the main room. Thunder's paws went *galumph galumph* on the floor as he ran to fling himself at me. "Thunder, Thunder, I missed you!" I knelt beside him and held him close. Obaachan tossed a few plastic-wrapped sandwiches onto the bed I was sharing with Jaz. Jaz had mayonnaise on his upper lip. He always squeezed his sandwiches too hard.

Then Obaachan stood next to the bed where Jiichan was sleeping. It was dim in the room. "He look terrible," she said. "He look gray." She scowled at me like it was all my fault. Then she nodded at nothing and continued sadly, "I guess this last time we work for Parkers. I know I give trouble to Mrs. Parker, but she good woman. They no hire us again. It my fault. I should have learn to drive combine. I should have take better care of my back. I should have done yoga. I should have brought *umeboshi* for Toshi." She hung her head low and nodded once more.

I didn't know what to say. I called softly to Thunder and stuck my DEET into a back pocket. We walked around the motel, down the highway, and back to the motel, thinking about the idea I'd had earlier. It felt good to move around in the clean night air. When I got back inside, everyone was asleep except Obaachan, who was sitting up on her bed with a table lamp weakly glowing. She didn't speak to me.

I lay with my back facing her and my eyes open, willing myself to stay awake. I heard movement, and the light turned off. It was pitch-black. Behind me Obaachan seemed to have finally lain down. Thunder hopped onto the bed and lay pressed against me. I counted to a thousand in my head. "Obaachan?" I said. She grunted in reply, but I thought she was only half awake, or maybe more like a quarter awake.

My heart was beating hard. As quietly as I could, I got out of bed, Thunder following. It was so dark, I kept my hands raised in front of me and moved slowly. I felt around for my flip-flops at the door. I had kept my keycard in my shorts pocket, so I was able to just slip outside. The temperature was pleasant, maybe mid-seventies. A wind blew in my face. I hesitated. It sure was dark out there beyond the motel! I made up my mind and stepped off the curb.

I wished I had a flashlight. There was the flashlight in the combine, but that didn't help me now. The motel sign blinked unsteadily. No vacancies. I loved the light. It made me feel safer. I knew Thunder could see, but for me it was kind of scary. There was a slight illumination toward the road, so I headed that way. I heard a thump and cried out. Then I stood perfectly still and listened. I didn't hear anything more. So I continued to the road. When I got there, I saw that the illumination came from what looked like some kind of warehouse-y building, with a flag out front. Still, it was so dark. Then Thunder ran off and disappeared in the night. I froze. "Thunder, come!" He ran back and nudged my hand.

In the distance the combines from the other farm threw more smidgeons of light my way. Thankfully, the headlights were facing me, so the light kept growing as I kept slowly moving forward. "We're going to save the day," I said to

Thunder. "That's what we're doing, in case you're wondering." And then I wondered if I was dreaming all this.

I thought about how my father had sat with me when I'd operated the combine at the Hillbinkses' farm back home. And now he was far away. Far, far away. It would be daytime in Japan now.

I suddenly felt sick with worry. What if I damaged the combine somehow? I thought about that $350,000 they cost. I wasn't sure exactly how I could damage a combine—there weren't any trees or big rocks or anything on the Franklin farm for me to hit, but still . . .

Relief flooded through me when I finally saw the headlights from Mick's combine. I could make out where the other combine was parked. "There it is, boy! Hurray!" I jogged forward, surrounded by the din of a seeming army of crickets.

When I reached the combine, I pressed my cheek against the cool, soothing metal. I pushed Thunder up before scrambling up myself, closing the door, and getting behind the wheel.

Then, suddenly, *unhhh*. My insides felt like they were all squishing around, as if everything inside of me was trying to change places or something. Ugh. I closed my eyes and took a few big breaths. But I didn't have a choice. I felt along the floor for the flashlight and set it next to me. I honked the horn twice, even though I knew nobody but Mick was out there. I turned the key in the ignition and switched on the lights.

The radio crackled immediately. "Toshiro?" Mick asked.

I picked up the radio. "It's me, Summer."

"Summer! What are ya doing?"

"I'm going to drive the combine. I know how." Sort of. I sort of knew how.

There was a long pause, so long that I almost asked him if he was still there. Then he said, "Are ya sure, then?"

"Yes, I've done it before. It was a breeze."

"There's no such thing as a breeze in life," he replied, but he didn't say more.

I put the combine into second gear and released the parking brake, then eased the machine toward the wheat beyond. The radio came on again.

"Why don't ya take the north and I'll take the south?"

"Okay," I said smoothly. But my brain was saying, *North? Which way is north?* But then I remembered where the sun had set. So that was west.

I drove at two miles per hour to the edge of the uncut wheat. I engaged the separator by pushing the button down and up. Then I engaged the header button, which was located right beside the main drive—both yellow buttons that you pushed down and forward. I wasn't even sure what all these buttons were for. I just did what my dad had taught me.

Once everything was engaged and running, the combine vibrated, and I knew something big was happening. I then lowered the header with the right-hand control. Next I pushed the hydro handle, and a hydraulic propulsion motor moved the machine forward. It made it very easy to slowly push the lever to the right just a tad and then forward. I could have pushed farther forward for a faster speed, but I was too scared.

I kept my left hand on the steering wheel and my right hand on the headers' height-control button. Like I said earlier, the field was terraced. I had to be very sensitive to the ground. It was kind of like when you're walking and you automatically adjust your feet with each step. My queasiness was gone, and I felt more alert than I'd ever felt. It was like all my senses were amped. I could even smell better, my nostrils filling with the scent of wheat. I pushed the lever up to four miles per hour.

"Don't go too fast," Mick's voice boomed over the radio.

I was feeling annoyed with Mick and didn't answer him. He was just a negative person. But I did feel a little out of control, so I slowed back down to two miles per hour. Even safe in the cab and slathered with DEET, I worried about mosquitoes. They had an amazing sense of smell. But then I thought how they could fly only one or one and a half miles an hour. So if they were chasing me, they couldn't catch me in the combine. That was probably pretty illogical, but it made me feel better. It wasn't a fair fight because they could use senses scientists didn't even understand. They could see a hot body, smell my sweat, and smell my exhaled breath from a hundred feet away, all of which got them really excited. And take it from me, you don't want to get a mosquito excited.

Now I felt a strange pressure all over my body. And the pressure on my insides seemed so intense that my chest hurt. Something started squeezing my heart and lungs. Who ever heard of a twelve-year-old girl having a heart attack? I knew I wasn't having one, but my chest did hurt, and I thought for a moment that maybe it was a rare young-girl heart attack. I remembered Obaachan saying pressure was the most powerful force in the world. I had a lot of pressure on me and in me.

After driving for five minutes, I idled the combine to calm down. The control panel said the bin was at 40 percent capacity, just a little more than what Jiichan had filled the bin with. If I went two miles an hour and cut 7.5 acres an hour, then . . . Argh! I couldn't figure it out just now. Anyway, who cared? *Just drive.*

I began driving again. I could feel my insides warm up, like I had just drunk hot apple cider. It was only me. Driving a combine on my own! And it was working. Dust filled the air, and I turned on the windshield wipers. I put my whole attention—everything I had—on what

I was doing. The only other time I had ever focused this much was when I was holding Jaz still during one of his outbursts.

I was doing good. I knew it. I couldn't see Mick because of the dust, but then he suddenly appeared out of nowhere, and we passed each other going in opposite directions. The controls said the combine was filling. When I reached 50 percent, it kind of seemed like a miracle. I happily watched the header turn around and around as it cut.

Time seemed to be moving so slowly. I could walk faster than two miles per hour. It was taking forever for the combine to fill. But the readout said it was getting fuller. Then, finally, unbelievably, it was full. I raised the header. The combine could turn on a dime. I made a U-turn and headed for the big rig.

I pulled up close to it and pressed the auger-out button to release the auger. As the controls indicated that my combine was emptying, I leaned back and closed my eyes. I felt so gratified and excited. Me, Summer, I was doing this! I leaned over and hugged Thunder. Suddenly, Mick cried out over the radio. "Summer, ya're missing the trailer! Stop dumping!"

"What!" I jabbed the button to stop the dumping, then scrambled onto the platform.

No. It couldn't be. I was paralyzed with panic. There was a pile of wheat on the ground. I couldn't think what I should do besides stand there and stare.

When my brain started working again, I rushed into the cab and brought in the auger. I leaned over the steering wheel to compose myself. I was here. Now. And I couldn't escape. I had pulled up my combine a few inches too short of the grain trailer.

I didn't want to go out and see exactly how much wheat I had spilled. I didn't want to, but I had to. Obaachan, the Parkers, Mick, Mr. Franklin—they would all be furious at me. And Jiichan would be very disappointed. Then I remembered Jiichan's advice: If you ever do something bad, you have to try to hurry through it, get it over with.

I turned off the ignition, grabbed the flashlight, and pushed open the door. I paused to enjoy one more second of not seeing up close what I had done. Then I descended a couple of steps down the ladder and jumped down the rest of the way, Thunder following. I could smell the cut wheat. Ordinarily, that would be a good smell, except now what I was smelling was spilled wheat, wheat I had let fall to the ground. I kept thinking over and over that I couldn't escape. Then I saw it: a mountain of wheat on the ground. I leaned against the combine, pushing back tears, then climbed quickly back into the cab and picked up the radio. "Mick?"

"What, Summer?"

"It's terrible!" I said. "There's so much wheat on the ground!" My voice sounded squeaky.

"Be right there."

I rushed down again. The combine's headlights lit up the night, cutting sharp shadows into the field. The pile of fallen wheat seemed to be taunting me.

I wished I could hurry through this, but at the moment there was nothing to do. I stared at the pile. It looked like about twenty or thirty bushels. The farmer would blow a gasket if he saw his precious wheat spilled. He spent the entire year working toward this moment!

When Mick reached me, he quickly assessed the situation. "Looks like about sixty bushels," he said. It was even worse than I'd thought!

"I have to lie down for a second," I said. I lay in the fetal position. In the scheme of things, this wasn't so bad, was it? Wars were worse. Getting hurt was worse. Malaria was worse. I closed my eyes. I didn't want to see anything. I tried to concentrate on not seeing the usual mess of shapes in my head. I just wanted darkness and peace. Instead I saw the header turning through the wheat. I could hear its roar as well. It almost felt as if I would never see or hear anything else.

I pushed myself up and waited for Mick to tell me how stupid I was. He said crisply, "Not to worry. Not to worry. I'll get the shovel from the pickup. All I need to do is shovel the wheat onto the header and turn on the combine. But we'll have to pick up the rest by hand. That's what'll take the time." He stared at the spilled wheat for a second before repeating, "That's what'll take the time." He jogged toward the pickup but stopped to call out, "Ya move the header closer to the wheat."

I grunted as I pushed and lifted Thunder up to the combine's platform. I didn't want him loose where he might get caught in the header. I climbed up after him and backed up the combine so the header was closer to the spilled grain. When I turned off the combine again, I just sat up there as Mick plunged the shovel into the wheat, again and again and again.

I wished there were some sand around, so I could stick my head under it. My life just stank, totally and completely. I was nothing but a nuisance. I leaned my head against the side window, and an overwhelming feeling of loneliness washed over me. Then I suddenly thought about Jaz, and I wondered if this was how lonely he felt almost all the time. That thought made me feel like throwing up.

I saw the stars, the sliver of the moon, and I thought wearily that tomorrow night I would be needed again. "Rise to the occasion!" my father sometimes shouted at an athlete on TV. That's what I had to do.

Mick stopped shoveling and signaled me to turn on the header. I complied, and then I turned off the combine as he started shoveling again. We did this over and over.

I eagerly clambered down to see if all the wheat was gone. I was pretty disappointed: There was still a very visible amount of wheat on the ground. The trailer was parked on a grassy area. It would have been better if the spill had happened in an area filled with cut straw. That way the wheat that remained on the ground wouldn't be so visible. The grains of wheat were about the size of grains of rice. The wheat looked terrible lying there in the grass. Mr. Franklin would be furious.

Mick kicked angrily at the ground and muttered something under his breath. "We got three-quarters of it up—we'll have to leave this for now," he then said to me. "The time that it'll take to pick up the rest is better spent driving the combines. We need to maximize the amount of wheat we can save for Franklin. Look, the trailer will be almost full by the time I dump my load. I was almost full when I called ya. So let me dump, then we'll clean the combines and call it a night. I'm too banjaxed to keep cutting." Mick ran a hand through his hair. "Ahhh. I'll clean yers as well or maybe I'll skip it. Why don't ya go back to the motel."

He didn't seem annoyed with me, I realized with relief. "Thank you," I said.

"It's all my job."

"Still, thank you. Good night." I couldn't believe he didn't want to kill me.

"Summer, don't worry," he said kindly. "Ya did a decent job cutting."

I watched him walk back to his combine and then honk twice, though who would be out there this time of night I didn't know. I wondered how much longer Mick would be up working. It seemed like a thousand years ago that I had thought he was a negative person; now I wished he was my big brother.

As I walked back to the motel, the town was silent, the highway empty. Thunder ran back and forth across the road. I felt much more confident with the flashlight, and I broke into a jog.

When I reached the motel office, I could see that a television was on somewhere inside. I could hear a humming noise from the fluorescent lights by the vending machines. I bought water, and I sat on the curb for a moment with Thunder, laying my head on my knees and crying. I cried because I was relieved the night was over and also because I knew I had to go back out there tomorrow and run the combine again.

# CHAPTER FIFTEEN

I slipped quietly into our room and took a shower, not just to clean myself, but to wash the pressure out from inside me. Showers had a way of doing that, of washing you inside and out. When I got out of the shower, I just about went to pieces: My left leg itched. I reached down to scratch and felt a mosquito bite. A mosquito bite! It took all of my willpower not to start screaming. I squatted down to peer at the bite and had the strangest thought.

I remembered that it had taken a couple of weeks after the bite that gave me malaria to start feeling sick. So even if this mosquito bite I had now really was from an infected mosquito, which was pretty close to impossible, I'd still have time to work the combine for Jiichan tomorrow and finish up this job with Mick before it was too late. But I didn't want to think about tomorrow. I opened the bathroom door and climbed in bed next to Jaz, pulling the sheet over my head for a mosquito net.

"Obaachan?" I said softly.

"What you want?"

"Nothing." Had I woken her up, or did she really never sleep?

Then somehow it was light out, and I was alone in the room. Where was everybody? I checked the clock—it was ten already. Had I just dreamed the previous night, or had it really happened? Obaachan had let me sleep in!

I lay in bed thinking, trying to figure it all out. There was Obaachan the ogre, and there was Obaachan who let me sleep late. There was Obaachan who scolded me night and day, and there was Obaachan who did as much of the cooking as she could, despite her pain, so I wouldn't have to. There was Obaachan who supposedly lived at the hospital when I was sick, and there was Obaachan who taunted me for, well, for everything. I mean, there was only one me, one Jaz, one Mom, one Dad, and one Jiichan. But it seemed like there were two Obaachans—the good one and the bad one.

I got up, slathered on DEET, and pulled on my only long-sleeved shirt and a pair of jeans—I wanted as much of my body covered as possible, even though most mosquitoes were nocturnal. Then I grabbed some one-dollar bills from my purse for the vending machine. When I stepped outside, the heat hit me hard. Jaz and a boy I'd never seen were sitting in the shade doing something—it looked like arranging gravel. I bought iced tea and trail mix at the vending machines and eagerly tore open the trail mix. Blech. It tasted just as old as the one I'd eaten before.

I sat down next to Jaz. "How is Jiichan?" I asked.

"Same," Jaz said without looking at me. He was studying a single piece of gravel; for whatever crazy reason, he rejected it and chose another. He placed the new piece into the arrangement they were making. The arrangement looked like lace—perfect lace.

"You mean he's still really sick?"

"Maybe a little better." Then Jaz lifted his head and evaluated me like a detective. "Something's fishy," he said. "What are you up to?

"What?"

Then he lost interest in me and turned back to his gravel. "What did they say?" I asked.

"Who?" Jaz held up a piece of gravel for his companion to inspect. "What do you think?"

The other boy looked up, but he didn't glance my way. He watched Jaz set the piece into the lace. "Cool," he said.

"Obaachan and Jiichan, what did they say?"

"What do you mean? Say when?"

"About me sleeping so late or about anything."

"Nothing."

I looked really closely at the lace. It was gorgeous, like something you would see in Queen Elizabeth's room. "Where is Obaachan?"

"She's riding with Jiichan because he's still sick or she's at the elevator," Jaz said impatiently. He wanted to concentrate on his gravel. The other boy just stared at the ground too.

I knew that Obaachan's back would hurt even more than usual tonight because of how uncomfortable the passenger seat was in the combine. And they had no real food. I squinted toward the sky. There were clouds gathering, but they weren't yet rain clouds. Since Jiichan was still sick, I definitely would be needed again tonight. I tried to figure out how that made me feel, and it came to me: determined. I imagined going three miles per hour, even four. But actually, I didn't want to go faster. Two was fine.

"That's pretty," I told Jaz, pointing to the arrangement.

He squinted at me with scorn, either because I was bothering him or because he didn't like me calling his work "pretty."

He returned to his project. The amazing thing was how even the spaces were, how perfect the curves. It was really beautiful. A touch of envy rose inside me. He was so, so good at things. Ridiculous things, maybe, but couldn't he transfer that perfectionism to anything he wanted when he grew up? And who was this other boy? I could hardly tell the difference between his work and Jaz's. And they'd found each other in a small town in Oklahoma. That reminded me of something Jiichan had once said: "You find magic every-where, in wheat field, in mosquito, even here." When he'd said that, we were driving through the town of Lost Springs, Wyoming, which had a population of four. Jaz and I were making fun of it, and Jiichan had cautioned us to stop laugh-ing. "Don't make fun. You don't know what magic here. Maybe bad magic, maybe good."

"Do you get an endorphin rush doing that?" I asked Jaz. "Remember endorphins from Obaachan's acupuncture?" We'd once gone to Wichita with her to get acupuncture for her back, and the acupuncturist had said that when the needles were placed just right, you got a rush of something inside you that made you feel good. That something was called "endorphins."

"I remember," he said, as if annoyed that I was still there. "What does gravel have to do with endorphins?"

I leaned back again. The pattern was about four feet long by two feet wide. But what was its purpose? Shoot, if I could make a lace pattern like that, well, I wouldn't be wasting my time making a lace pattern like that. I'd be . . . doing something—not sure exactly what.

Jaz looked at the intricate arrangement one last time and stood up. Then, with his foot, he wiped away the gravel. That startled me. All that work destroyed in an instant. "Come on," he said to the boy. They walked away, then the two of them stood facing the door to our motel room.

"I don't have a key," Jaz said to me.

I held up mine, and he came and got it without speaking. The boys went inside the room. Obviously, they didn't want me in their little gravel-arranging club. I decided to try to make some lace of my own. I know I had just gotten through saying it was a waste of time, but I wanted to see if I could do it. Though there was no physical exertion involved, soon I was sweating profusely. It was like working my brain was causing me to sweat. I got really involved with making the lace. It was so hard for me to make my lines perfect, and when I stepped away, I saw how uneven it all was.

After a while I bought a bottle of water from the machine and said to Thunder, "Water." He stretched his neck and opened his mouth as I poured in a small amount at a time. He was as much of a genius as Jaz was, just in a different way.

I sat back down. I was going to make beautiful lace. If I could drive a combine, I could do this. For hours I sat there arranging the gravel into lace, occasionally stopping to eat stale trail mix, drink iced tea, and give Thunder water. By two p.m., my T-shirt was soaked and my hair was matted with perspiration. Thunder was panting. And my lace still didn't look half as good as Jaz's.

My back ached from leaning over. I lay down and stared at the awning above me. I could really see why Obaachan liked to lie down flat on her back. It felt great. Thunder got up and put his nose on my face to make sure I was okay.

"I'm a failure at arranging gravel," I told him. He licked my face. "I give up." I pushed myself up with a groan and went to the door to our room. When I knocked, Jaz didn't answer. I knocked harder. The door opened, and on the floor were a bunch of LEGOs arranged into a lace pattern.

With the boys hard at work, my mind wandered back to *A Separate Peace*, to how Finny had died. The weird thing about dying is that while you're doing it, you're not afraid of it, but the second you're not doing it, you're scared of it again. So did that mean it was scary or not scary? I started reading the book again.

An hour later the door opened, and Obaachan and Jiichan walked in. "We have dinner now," she said. The clock read 3:07 p.m. "We starving."

Jiichan lay down in the bed. Apparently, he wasn't joining us.

Jaz turned to his friend. "Wanna come?"

"Sure."

"Don't you have to ask your mother or

something?" I said to the boy. He looked maybe a year younger than Jaz, with dark hair and faded blue eyes.

"She's cutting today. So's my dad."

Mick was waiting outside, and we all went to the front desk to get a restaurant recommendation. They said I should talk to the desk clerk because I spoke American English the best. Miss Talk So Good. I went into the empty office and leaned on the counter. "Hello?" I called. Nobody answered, so I gave the desk bell a short tingle. When nobody came, I gave it a firmer ring.

An older man walked in, looking almost confused. It was possible he hadn't talked to anyone all day.

"We were wondering if you could give us a restaurant recommendation."

He looked as if he was thinking. Finally, he said, "There's not that much to choose from. I guess Monty's is best. It has decent food for the money."

That wasn't much of an endorsement, but if that was the best place in town, so be it. He told me where Monty's was, and we drove in the pickup to the other side of town. Monty's was a buffet—fajitas and meat loaf and macaroni and cheese, among other entrées. The macaroni and cheese looked like it was dry on the outside, so I took the fajitas. I knew you couldn't go wrong with fajitas. All you had to do was fry up some meat and vegetables.

Well, the fajitas tasted awful. I wouldn't even know what to do to make fajitas taste that bad. It was almost like the person who cooked it must have had a special talent for bad cooking. There were some kind of crazy spices involved that I wasn't familiar with, but they didn't fit together. It was kind of like putting salt into iced tea or something. The spices just didn't make sense. The cost was $7.99 per person. So far it didn't seem worth it. On the other hand, it was slightly better than the trail mix and it did stop my hunger pangs. "How's the mac and cheese?" I asked Jaz.

He didn't answer because sometimes when Jaz was eating, he didn't hear you; he was focusing too hard on his food.

"The mac and cheese," I said again. "How is it?"

"I'm thinking," he said. "I can't find the words."

"This not food," Obaachan said.

"What is it?" I asked.

"I don't know," she replied. "Let's see. It not plastic. It not clay. It not mud. It not wax." She looked at me. "You ask good question. I need to think about."

"I've been thinking," said Jaz's friend. "Maybe we should try to build the Eiffel Tower with your LEGOs."

"Good idea," Jaz said.

I decided to clean my plate because I knew it would be a long night. Also, I had been on harvest before, so I knew you just had to eat your restaurant food and accept it.

Mick was mostly quiet. The Irish guys talked more when they were all together. They were kind of shy that way. Then I thought about it and realized that we didn't talk much in front of the Parkers either. It's hard to have a big conversation with people who are in charge of you sixteen hours a day.

As always, Obaachan was eating with her whole fist wrapped around her fork. Jiichan always ate that way too. I thought I'd try it now, and I discovered it was easier for me to eat that way than the proper way. Then Obaachan's gaze fell on me. Her mouth opened, but before she could say anything, I started to hold the fork the right way. She closed her mouth and returned to her food.

After we finished, we stepped out into the warm air. Mick said, "I suppose I'm only going to feel the hot side of America, aren't I?"

"Very hot on harvest," Obaachan said politely. She was carrying leftovers home for Jiichan.

Obaachan dropped Mick at the farm, then drove us to the motel. "Tomorrow I go to store and make sandwich for Mick," Obaachan said.

On the TV was a show about cooking fancy food. It had absolutely no relevance at all to how we cooked on harvest. The cook lady was neatly arranging food on a platter. The boys seemed fascinated, so I didn't change the channel.

I heard Jiichan and Obaachan talking quietly together. Then Obaachan announced, "Now I know what they feed at restaurant. Your *jiichan* explain. When you put the hate in food you cook, person who eat die. When you put love, person stronger. Mr. Monty put apathy into his food. I learn new word today: apathy. I think maybe Mr. Monty put two or three apathy in his food."

Once Jiichan fell asleep, Obaachan set off back to the fields to drive the semi to the elevator. I so wanted to work the combine now, instead of spending time cooped up in a musty motel room. But Obaachan would kill me so bad if she knew I'd driven last night, and she would kill me even worse if she knew I'd dropped a mountain of wheat, so I had no choice but to sneak out again late tonight after everyone else was asleep.

When the boys lost interest in the cooking channel, they got busy with their Eiffel Tower project. To start, the other boy drew a picture of the tower. It wasn't museum quality, but it was pretty darn good. Then the boys stared at the picture, as if they were meditating. The other boy even closed his eyes, maybe picturing the tower in his mind. I wished we could take him home with us. Jaz would never be lonely again.

They focused intently on their tower, occasionally discussing technical details. Finally, around nine p.m., the other boy said, "I better get back. My parents should be coming in around now. See you tomorrow."

"Sure," Jaz said.

They high-fived each other. I stood outside to make sure the boy got to his room okay. "What's his name?" I asked Jaz when I got back in.

"I don't know."

"You spent all that time with him and you don't know his name?"

"It didn't come up."

"Well, did he ask you your name?" I asked.

"Like I said, it didn't come up."

"But finding out someone's name is one of the first things you do when you meet."

"Says who?"

I just looked at him for another moment and then gave up. It was none of my business how he made friends.

Obaachan returned in a couple of hours and immediately lay on the floor. I did a double take when I saw a tear slide down the side of her face. Or was it perspiration?

"Obaachan, are you okay?" I asked.

"No bothering me," she answered sharply. "Go to sleep before I ground you."

"What would you ground me for?"

She didn't answer, which wasn't like her. I felt really kind of disturbed by that teardrop, if it was a teardrop. I didn't understand what was going on.

I took all my books and binders into the bathroom at once, but I didn't open any of them. I stayed in there for what seemed like a long, long time, brushing the knots out of my hair, trimming my toenails—anything I could think of to pass the time. I spread on yet more DEET, even though by doing so I broke a number of the EPA's rules for DEET, as usual. Here are the rules I broke:

- Read and follow all directions and precautions on this product label.
- Use just enough repellent to cover exposed skin and/or clothing.
- Do not use under clothing.
- Avoid overapplication of this product.
- Do not spray in enclosed areas.

And later I would break this one: After return-ing indoors, wash treated skin with soap and water.

Hopefully I would stop being scared of mos-quitoes before I perished from DEET exposure.

Anyway, about twenty minutes after I heard the TV go off, I tiptoed into the room. "Jaz?" No answer.

"Jiichan?" No answer.

"Obaachan?" Not even a grunt.

Making sure I had my keycard and the flash-light, I slipped out the door with Thunder.

# CHAPTER SIXTEEN

The walk sure was less scary with the flashlight. When I climbed into my combine, I immediately picked up the radio. "I'm here," I said to Mick.

"Summer" was all he said.

"Yep, it's me."

"Be careful when ya dump tonight."

"I will. Mick?"

"Yes?"

"Thank you for helping me yesterday." And in my head I was also apologizing to him for not liking him before and wishing he had fallen out of a truck.

"It was nothing."

Thunder lay squished at my feet as I honked twice and started the combine. I started to feel like we were in our own world. I felt safe, the way Jaz felt safe in his bed at home. He loved his bed. I knew this because he kept all his important possessions on the shelf in his headboard at home. He kept a key from when we had lived in another house he liked better. He kept his completed Sudoku books. And he kept a box of his favorite LEGO minifigs.

I suddenly realized I was thinking about something else and operating the combine at the same time. According to my controls, the moisture content of the wheat was 11.5 percent: still perfect. Thunder whimpered in a dream. Mick was wrapped in dust on the far end of the field.

I could drive confidently at two miles per hour, but when I tried three, everything seemed barely under control. Two was good.

When I needed to pee, I stopped the combine and slipped into an area facing the empty highway. When I got back, Mick was on the radio. "Everything all right?"

"Yes," I replied. Then I added, "Ten-four,"

because I had learned that from a movie. I pushed yesterday's mistake out of my mind. Like Jiichan sometimes said to Jaz when Jaz got stuck on something, "Walk on, walk on." And at least it seemed as though the farmer hadn't noticed.

The bin was empty when I started. I drove slowly, sometimes even more slowly than two miles an hour. I wanted it to fill, and yet I didn't want it to. I wished the combine would break down. Then I wouldn't have to dump, and the Parkers couldn't get mad. Mick had already dumped twice by the time my bin was filled.

I drove over to the semi. I thought about my whole life. There wasn't that much to think about, except that I'd had malaria. I was born in Kansas, and I still lived in Kansas. I went to school. I hated homework. My mother was lenient, my grandmother was strict. I got three dollars a week for an allowance.

I moved the auger over the grain trailer. Then I turned off the combine and got out to stand on the platform. The auger was over the trailer but very close to the edge. I got back into the cab, honked twice, and started the engine again. I pulled in the auger, backed up, and moved closer to the semi, feeling a little sick to my stomach about how close I was. I knew that the famous John Deere green color on this combine was polished and perfect, and I didn't want to be the one to scratch it. But when I got out to check, the combine wasn't as close as I had feared.

I pushed the auger-out button located on the throttle control, and then I pushed one more button on the throttle lever, this one a bit harder to reach, so you didn't accidentally hit it and lose the grain while you were driving in the field. A beeper sounded the whole time I was dumping. The beep was to tell the operator that the auger was running. When the controls said that my combine was empty, I pressed the same button. Then I brought the auger back in by pressing the auger-return button. I realized I was holding my breath. I exhaled, then inhaled deeply, smelling the beautiful scent of cut wheat.

I picked up the radio. "I did it! I dumped my whole load, and it's perfect!" I said to Mick excitedly.

"Good girl!" he answered. "Can ya get that

wee section near ya? The field is a strange shape, isn't it?"

"Got it," I said. "Ten-four."

That was it. I was a combine driver, or maybe a third of one since I went so slowly. I tried to do that math in my head, and for once I could think clearly. Since I went two miles an hour and good drivers went five miles an hour, that meant I was 40 percent of a combine driver, more or less. Not bad for a twelve-year-old girl.

"Summer."

I picked up the radio. "Yes?"

"I'm going to have to dump at the elevator. They're open late because of the rain this weekend. Do ya want to come with me or are ya okay by yerself?"

I didn't answer at first. I searched inside myself and decided that my need to keep cutting trumped my fear of being alone.

"Summer?"

"No, I'll be fine working out here."

But a minute after he drove off my heart started to go *whompa, whompa.* I was suddenly terrified out there by myself. I idled the combine and watched as the big rig's taillights disappeared in the distance. I sat very still, then turned off the ignition. I laid my arms on the steering wheel and my face on my arms, and pressed my eyes closed. I was so, so scared. I remembered a night several years earlier when I had a dog who was killed by a truck on the highway, and as I held him I thought I was going to lose my mind. That's kind of the way I felt right then, like everything that was real—the black sky and the stars and the wheat—all started to kind of melt into one another, and the only thing that seemed clear was me and a dog. *Whompa, whompa.* "Thunder, help me. I'm scared," I said, looking at him. He lifted his head curiously, then sat up and placed his paw on my leg.

I suddenly burst into sobs, and the next thing I knew, I wasn't sobbing because I was scared, but because my grandparents worked so hard and because Jaz couldn't make a friend at school and because I knew how desperately my parents wished for their own business, and I doubted they would ever get their wish.

I squeezed onto the floor and hugged Thunder

CYNTHIA KADOHATA

to me. As I hugged him something unfamiliar welled up inside of me. Maybe it was courage. I mean, this was *my* world, the black sky and the stars and the wheat. I knew this world backward and forward and up and down. I got back into my seat and looked around at the wheat. Something started to happen: The dust of my personality started to settle, and my fear left me. In its place was the hyper-superalertness from yesterday.

I turned on the ignition and got back to work.

When my bin was full, Mick still hadn't returned. I turned off my combine and waited for him.

He got back in an hour and called me on the radio. "I'm back. There was a bit of a line at the elevator. Are ya full?"

"Yes."

"I'll dump for ya. Why don't ya go on back to the motel? I'm thinking of quitting myself."

"Do you want me to help you clean the combines?"

"Naw. Go get yer sleep."

"Okay, 'night!" I said. And that's when excitement flooded into me. I hadn't made any mistakes today! I wanted to jump up and touch the sky.

I parked the combine where I had found it and walked home.

One of my flip-flops broke, so I walked barefoot in the middle of the road to avoid stepping on gravel. I walked exactly in the middle because that somehow made me feel kind of like I was celebrating or in a movie or something. I was so happy. I loved how quiet it was out, how the breeze brushed my face, and how the road felt soft under my feet. Bugs touched my face like snowflakes.

When I reached the motel, I snuck into the room. Even Obaachan seemed to be fast asleep. I changed into a T-shirt without showering—too bad, EPA!—and eased myself into bed beside Jaz. Thunder jumped on top of me. An hour went by. I couldn't sleep. I felt wired. I gave up trying to sleep, got my keycard, and went to sit outside and look at the stars. Thunder followed me out.

I was startled to see Mick sitting on the curb down the way. "You finished cleaning the combines?" I asked.

He shook his head no. "I ran out of water."

He held up a couple of bottles of water from the vending machine. He took a swig and said, "Ya did good tonight. Yer grandparents are going to think I'm Superman when it comes to cutting."

"Thank you."

He sighed heavily, then looked up toward the stars and sighed again. "When my girl still loved me, she made me a quilt of the constellations. She's handy with a sewing machine."

I didn't reply.

"I wanted to marry her."

"She doesn't love you anymore?"

He shook his head again. He seemed really sad and rubbed his palms over his face and into his hair.

I didn't know what to say. I didn't know much about that stuff, except from my brief experience with Robbie. "I'm sorry."

"Don't be sorry, then. Being on a different continent has taken my mind off her quite a bit." He stood up and stretched. "I best be finishing my work."

"Okay, then good night," I said.

"Get some sleep."

I went inside, but I peeked back outside and saw Mick had sat back down. A few thin clouds passed in front of the moon. Soon it would rain. I hoped we would finish the field in time. If we did, it would be because of me, partly. I smiled a little smile and immediately felt guilty about being happy when Mick was so sad. I gently pushed the door shut.

I took a few silent steps.

A voice came out of the darkness. "You wake me up." Jiichan.

"I'm sorry," I said. "I tried to be quiet."

"When sick, not much difference between asleep and awake."

"Are you still really sick?"

"You use word 'really.'" He thought a moment. "No. I still sick, but not 'really.'"

"A little better?"

"Yes, I think a little better."

"I just stepped out for some fresh air. Mick was sitting out there, so we talked a little. I'm sorry I woke you up."

"I felt you walk in. No hear you. That woke me up."

"Obaachan was crying earlier," I blurted out.

"She been very sad."

"Because of all our bad luck?" I asked.

"No. Today in combine she say you growing up so fast, and she no could stop crying."

I stared at him for a moment. What did that mean?

Just then Obaachan chuckled in her sleep, no doubt over a dream of *America's Funniest Home Videos*. She said that was the only thing she ever dreamed of. Then something else about growing up occurred to me.

"Jiichan, can you be in love when you're only twelve?" I asked suddenly.

"You can be in love, but it the kind of love that go away, not kind that stay."

"How come it doesn't stay?"

"Why? You want to get marry?"

I thought this over. "No, I guess not yet. I mean, not for, like, twenty years. But . . . can't you be in love and not want to get married?"

I heard him making a small noise in his throat. When he was thinking really hard, sometimes he made a soft, squeaky sound. "Temporary love very beautiful thing. In Japan, thing that don't last called *tsukanoma*. *Tsukanoma* very beautiful, like cherry blossom. Perfect."

Jiichan paused. "*Wabi-sabi* beautiful too, in different way." Once, Jiichan had made me watch a BBC show about *wabi-sabi* that he'd recorded. It's very hard to determine what *wabi-sabi* is, because supposedly if you could define it, then you knew it couldn't really be *wabi-sabi*. It's kind of important to what it means to be Japanese, and yet hardly anybody knows exactly what it was. It kind of means that there can be beauty and nobility inside of a rough exterior. "Another thing. When you get marry, it like great Shinto shrine of Ise. It many hundreds of years old, but for all those hundreds of years, they rebuild it every twenty years. In temporary love, no rebuilding."

"If I tell you something, do you promise not to tell Obaachan?"

"I make solemn promise."

"I think I was in temporary love with Robbie Parker."

"First time I in love was Akiko. I same age as you."

267

"How long did you stay in love?"

"Five week. I never speak word to her in life, but I in love."

"How come you stopped loving her?"

"Orchid interesting flower. Some cherry blossom last only one week. Orchid can live many month. She was like cherry blossom."

"You mean your love withered away?"

"No wither, it fall off tree."

"Why did it fall off the tree?"

"I don't know. Maybe wind blow it off."

Then, just for the nosy heck of it, I asked, "Do you love Obaachan?"

"God put us together. That bigger than love. I tell you story. Jaz, you listen?"

"Yep," Jaz answered.

"You're awake! You tricked me!"

"I didn't trick you. Nobody asked me if I was awake."

"Listen to story," Jiichan said. He cleared his throat. "One day my brother and me have many work to do. But we decide to run away for just one day. We get our fishing poles and go to lake. We catch many fish. Nice day—overcast, so we don't get hot, but not cold enough for sweater. Many day my brother and me fight, but this day we like best friend. Then we go home and say, 'Look at all the fish we catch!' We excited. But we didn't do our chores that day. My father get switch and hit our legs until we cry. My brother get hit more than me because he older. Altogether, my brother live almost seventy year—that equal more than twenty-five thousand day. I with him at bed when he die. He say to me, 'Remember that day we run away and go fishing?' I tell him I remember clearly. 'Wasn't that day fun?' he say. I say, 'Yes,' and then he die. *Oyasumi.*"

"*Oyasuminasai,* Jiichan," Jaz and I said.

I cracked the door again and peeked out. I could see Mick still sitting on the curb. I watched him a long time. Then he looked up at something in the distance, and I turned to see what it was. It was a pair of combines driving side by side, their headlights illuminating the night. He had come across the ocean to drive one of those and forget about a girl he loved. I felt surprised. What I felt surprised about was how beautiful hard work looked—the combines moving slowly in tandem, the moon hanging over the field. It was *wabi-sabi*.

I knew going out to talk to Mick now wouldn't make him feel better. A twelve-year-old girl didn't mean a hill of beans to him. I couldn't help. It was just like we couldn't help Jaz to make friends at school, and just like I couldn't change Jenson's life with a simple hello. Still, as my dad liked to say, "You do what you can do." Maybe I would talk to Jenson again. Maybe I would keep looking for friends for Jaz back home.

I got back into bed, and as soon as my head hit the pillow, I knew something: Our year of bad luck had ended. It had begun when I caught malaria, and it had ended here tonight. Maybe I'd known that earlier, and that was why I had walked down the middle of the highway so happily. Anyway, I needed to get some sleep, because I'd have another long night tomorrow. I closed my eyes and saw the header, spinning . . . spinning . . . spinning.